Future Memories Collection

Part One:
Hello, World

By Steven E. Parton

2013 Curious Apes Publishing—First Paperback Edition

www.curiousapespublishing.com

Cover Art by Devin White

Published in The United States of America

ISBN 978-0-9910088-1-0

"Your problem is how you are going to spend this one odd and precious life you have been issued. Whether you're going to spend it trying to look good and creating the illusion that you have power over people and circumstances, or whether you are going to taste it, enjoy it and find out the truth about who you are."

Anne Lamott

Dedicated:

To my family,
whose unconditional love gave me the courage to define
myself.

To my friends,
who were willing to entertain my musings and give me
honest feedback.

To you,
for your interest in literature and willingness to explore
new perspectives.

Singularity Industries:

Upgrading to the New You

The first question we always receive is: "What happens to my body?"

At Singularity Industries, we leave that answer up to you. Listed below are the options for you to choose from based upon your spiritual, philosophical, and financial needs.

1. *Twin Living: With this option you simply walk in alone, undergo a quick non-invasive procedure, then walk out with your perfect, metallic twin. This option is great for those who are just looking for a companion, or who simply want to know that their mind will live on once they're gone.*

    Note: You are responsible for the well-being and livelihood of your twin.

    Note: Limited to one use per person. By Article 1, Section 2 of the Transhuman Articles of Existence, no consciousness may exist in more than two active capacities at once.

2. *Cryostasis: You're not going to need that old, fragile body once you move into You 2.0, but some people like holding on to their body for sentimental reasons. But don't worry—we'll take care of that by preserving your skin and bone body in our high-security, state-of-the-art storage facility. If you ever decide that being a machine just isn't for you, we'll restore your human flesh back to its original living state free of charge. We can even implant the memories of your android life into your brain for a nominal fee.*

3. *Trade-in: Here at SI, we want to make sure everyone has access to the next stage of human evolution, regardless of finances. To that end, we're happy to announce our newest promotion. If you don't want your old body after you make the switch, you can give it to us for research purposes, and we'll give you 25% off the total purchase price of You 2.0. You heard us right: that's 25% off your new body simply for giving us your old, outdated model. Not only are you saving money, but our researchers might just use your body to help save the world.*

CHAPTER ONE

Cece stood between two worlds: below was her home of comfort and stagnation, and on the horizon—past the ridge that protected her valley from the androids—was a place of danger and growth. She glanced down the hillside to the water tower that marked the hidden entrance to the Sanctuary; it seemed so far away.

The moss-covered mansion upon which she stood was the farthest she had ever been from her home. And, until an hour ago, it had also been the only building in the valley she hadn't been inside, the only building she hadn't rummaged through for parts.

There's no more, she realized with a sobering melancholy.

She had been everywhere now, had searched every building in the valley and explored every space in between. There were no more secrets to be found, no more jewels amongst the rubble that could give some insight into what life was like before the virus had cleared the planet of her ancestors.

Soon, that wouldn't matter, she decided, feeling the

rigid corners of the microprocessor in her pocket digging into her thigh. Thanks to the hillside mansion's communication system, she now had the piece necessary to make a real attempt at awakening her android scout.

The thought drew her attention to the vast world of wonder beyond the valley, to the place she would send her most precious creation once it was complete. It was there where high-tech cities stood abandoned and where androids were the dominant beings. And if her robotic scout could confirm it was safe—that the androids were friendly and the virus was gone—she would finally be able to explore it herself. It thrilled her to think of what dormant secrets she could learn in the dead cities of her ancestors, of what neglected trinkets she could use to rebuild the first human settlement the earth had seen in at least a century.

But until then...

Her eyes returned to the water tower. She needed to get back to the Sanctuary soon, before the other Guardians realized she was gone. If they became curious, it wouldn't take long for them to perform an exhaustive search of the too-small bunker; and after what had happened to her sister, Cece knew the other Guardians would be furious if they found out she was still exploring the surface against their wishes.

She performed a quick stretch to bring life back to her muscles, using the opportunity to indulge one last time in the rare view, in the rich green canopy that blanketed the valley and the infinite blue sky that seemed to make her body feel lighter, more free. She couldn't understand why the Guardians had decided they all should live in a concrete box when they could just as easily guard the database of souls from the surface; then she would be able to enjoy such awe-inspiring views whenever she wanted.

She gave a long, reluctant sigh. She didn't want to

leave the surface, not yet, but she told herself it would be worth it: the sooner she got back, the sooner she could test her newly acquired microprocessor inside the android. And so with bittersweet determination, she began her slow, cautious descent down to the valley floor, back to the hidden tunnel that would sneak her underground.

*

Cece crawled through the tunnel, both shoulders scrapping along the dirt edges of the earthen passageway. She pushed and pulled, mud packing thicker and thicker under her fingernails as she went.

She soon emerged into the wooden crate that acted as the hidden gateway between the tunnel and Sanctuary. Streaks of light from her workshop pierced through the cracks in the box and highlighted lines across her skin. She sat in complete silence for nearly a minute as she listened for any movement from within her workshop.

Nothing.

She pushed up the lid just enough to peer through, saw it was clear, then quickly climbed out. After closing the box, she gathered an armful of scraps from nearby and placed them on top.

She high-stepped over the clutter that filled her workshop, making her way over pile after pile of electronics, each one a project that reflected her tendency for overly-ambitious endeavors. The room was difficult to maneuver in, but she liked keeping her numerous projects in sight at all times, liked keeping herself constantly reminded of each small step she had taken to rebuild the splendor of her species. She was worried that if her creations were out of sight, then they would simply fade out of memory as well. Besides, there was no reason to clean—no one else used the room.

For the rest of the Guardians, the workshop was a scrapyard of garbage—a concept she couldn't understand, given that the room housed the most advanced technology the world had ever seen.

Towering in the center of the room, its tentacles of cords dangling from a body of monitors, was the Kernal—the terminal responsible for uploading human minds and copying them into machines. Nearby was the domed-covered chair that processed the uploading and the gurney on which her android lay inanimate and incomplete.

Cece felt saddened by its appearance as she approached, as though her creation was dead rather than merely non-functioning. Even though the artificial skin on its face was the only humanistic feature it had, the figure still radiated an essence of being. She ran her fingers across the arm of the metallic corpse and was overwhelmed by a sense of kinship. She found herself wondering if her consciousness, once inside the machine, would miss the sensation of true human touch, the feeling of skin on skin.

She quickly pushed the thought away. Now wasn't the time to worry about such things, not while the android was still inoperative. She needed to focus on the task on hand, and that meant finding out whether or not her latest code could be the thing that would finally give her scout a functioning body.

Cece retrieved the microprocessor from her pocket and stood against her workbench, taking the time to carefully solder the embedded systems—which she had already programmed—onto the new processor's surface. She then slid it into the skull of the android and stepped anxiously behind the Kernal.

She wished she could use the extraordinary machine for its primary purpose, but for now she would have to settle for its secondary function: testing the integrity of her android's framework. She rubbed her fingers over the name embossed on the machine: *Singularity Industries*—the company who had built the machine and the entire Sanctuary, the very facility that was responsible for saving her people from the Virus. She handled the ancient relic with a delicate touch as she turned it on, careful to avoid any damage to the one-of-a-kind machine. It was the most important thing in the world to her, even if no one else cared.

The thought sent a sudden spike of frustration through her as she awaited the machine to come on. All she could think about was how little her people cared for the beautiful machine that stood so majestically in front of her.

How could the last humans on the planet so willingly give up on progress? she wondered suddenly. *Why protect their precious database of souls if they never planned to do anything with it?*

Her people tried to explain it to her, told her she couldn't understand because she was so young; but she knew age wasn't a sign of wisdom, and at nineteen she felt she had already surpassed even the most wrinkled of her fellow Guardians in their understanding of the world.

They considered themselves divinely ordained to watch over the database, because that's what they wanted to believe. They called themselves Guardians—even called her one—but she knew they were more akin to squatters. They were simply people who had used the database of backed-up minds as an excuse to be complacent—as a false sense of purpose that could justify their apathetic existence.

The Kernal signaled the completion of its start-up process with a subtle beep. The screen suddenly blinked on and displayed a menu with half a dozen options. Cece carefully navigated her way through the on-screen buttons until the terminal rendered a flashing, silver icon that read: "Compile and Run."

The moment of truth, she thought. Once she pressed the

button she would know whether or not this metal vessel was ready to download a mind, or if it would remain little more than an amalgamation of scraps arranged in humanoid form.

Cece crossed her fingers on one hand, and hit the button with the other.

Several charts of analytics suddenly filled the screen: power usage, memory capacity, number of processes successfully running, number of processes failed, as well as a full-body schematic that used a simple green and red configuration to showcase functional and non-functional body parts. Amongst all the ever-changing data, she only watched the "number of processes failed" count, willing it to stay at zero. Her right foot slowly started to tap as she watched; not long after, her fingers found their way to her mouth where she nibbled at her fingernails. She caught herself in the midst of this nervous habit after several minutes, silently reprimanded herself for the action, fiddled with her watch momentarily, and then brought her hands to toy with the tiny gears that hung from her necklace instead.

A thousand files uploaded, each now a successfully running process. *So far, so good,* she thought. *Only fifty thousand left to go.*

Her record was 42,000, but every little change could throw off any file; one simple tweak to any power module or synthetic synapse could throw tens of thousands of other processes into a cascade of bugs and errors. She watched the number reach 17,000, and as it continued to climb, so too did her spirits.

"It's not going to work," a familiar voiced called out from behind.

"Not now, Curtis," Cece replied sternly.

Curtis arrived at her side; his lean 17 year-old frame and short black hair cast a shadow over her. "Staring at it won't help, ya know?"

She turned, breaking her willful concentration. "I said: Not. Now."

A beep sounded—faint, yet profound. Her hopes faded with its echo. She turned to the readout, already knowing what she would see—" Failed Processes: 37," and climbing. Cece leaned against the edge of the gurney the android rested upon and let out a sigh. *Another failure.*

"Told you," Curtis teased. "When are you going to give up on this and help me do something that could actually make a difference in the world? We don't need more robots, ya know, we need more humans."

Cece wanted to yell at him, to let him know it was about more than just another *robot*, that it was their only hope to finally explore and expand and learn...but she resisted the urge, knowing it was her fault the android wasn't working, not Curtis'. "I'll get it to work," she said. "Then you'll see how important this project *really* is. Besides, you need me to succeed, 'cause otherwise there's *no way* you'll be able to figure out how to finish your meat vessel."

Curtis snorted. "Actually, I've been making a ton of progress. I even managed to grow a synapse that can hold a binary just the other day."

Cecelia feigned wonder. "Wow...now all you have to do is get it to do that 100 trillion times more and then grow a full human body to put it all in. Be sure to revive me in a few hundred years so I can see it in action."

His face darkened. "At least *I'm* actually trying to help the Sanctuary," he said. "And maybe one day I'll be able to give the minds in the database a body—a *human* body."

"And why can't it be an android body?—you know...something that won't break or get sick...something that can survive another Virus."

"Because we're human, that's why—and those

consciousnesses—they're human, too. And that's what we need more of: humans, not more soulless computers with legs."

"They're not soulless. They can feel just like us."

"How would you know?"

"Because I read the manuals our ancestors left behind. Because I've written the programs that give them emotional capacity to feel pain and happiness. There is no difference between your synthetic cell and my electronics; they both do the same thing—they either trigger or they don't. Which means my droid would hold a soul from the database the same as your synthetic flesh would. That's what reverse engineering is...it's almost a perfect copy."

Curtis examined the scrapyard android on the cold steel slab—looked at its rough welds, exposed circuitry, and mismatched pieces—and laughed. "They don't seem perfect to me at all. And if they had souls, this . . . *thing . .* .would wake up when I did this." He knocked on its chest with a heavy fist; a dull thud sounded and the android remained unmoving. "But it doesn't."

He turned and fell into a confident lean against the gurney, coming to rest so that his and Cece's arms were pressed together as they stood.

Cece felt a wave of nervous excitement at his touch. She straightened suddenly, pulling away from the uncomfortable closeness, and leveled her gaze at him. "So did you come here just to bother me, Curtis? Because I've got a lot to do and I'm really not in the mood for—"

"Whoa," Curtis said, raising a hand in defense. "Relax. I just thought I'd come see if you wanted to get some lunch with me."

"I really don't think—"

"Come on, Cece. Take a break. When's the last time you ate—or even went to the lounge? It'll be good for your work to take a break for awhile. I know it always helps me with mine."

Cece weighed the decision logically. Going to the lounge meant surrounding herself with the rest of the Guardians, which sounded dreadful, but at least with Curtis there she would have someone to converse with; and it *had* been awhile since she had talked to anyone.

And she *was* hungry.

"Okay," she agreed half-heartedly. "But just for a bit."

They walked side by side in awkward silence through the bleak concrete hallways, only the echoes of their footsteps adding a tempo to their journey. Every so often they passed one of the black-matte, nanocarbon frames that hid blast-doors within, ready to slam shut in case of an emergency.

Wearing her favorite forest-green military jacket, and with the red filigree bandana holding back her dark hair, Cece felt as though she were a soldier walking through the bunker she called home; Curtis' clean-shaven, gentle face and soft golden complexion made him look more like a peacekeeper.

But the oppressive and decaying halls didn't make her think of peace; instead, they were a painful reminder of why she worked so hard. They reminded her that there was a whole world above her head—a surface world with infinite possibilities for growth and adventure—and that the sooner her android was up and running, the sooner it could explore beyond the valley of the Sanctuary and discover whether it was safe enough for her to explore herself.

"So everyone's saying you've stopped showing up for your duties at the gardens and at the dig," Curtis said, breaking the silence. "You know Kensington is going to say something if you don't start helping out soon."

"I know," Cece replied flatly.

"So don't you think you should start fulfilling your shifts?"

"I don't really have the time. I'm finally making some real progress towards finishing my droid and I'm not going to start slowing myself down now."

"Yeah, well you're not going to get to it finished if Kensington throws you out."

Cece sighed. "They're not going to throw me out, Curtis. I'm worth more to them than that."

"You sure?"

"We're the last of our kind. Do you really think they'd get rid of a perfectly good breeder because I haven't tossed a few shovels of dirt?" She shook her head. "I doubt it."

"I've heard differently."

She paused and gave him glaring stare. "From who?" Cece sneered. Such an idea would be news to her; then again, she didn't keep up with the rumors.

"Just around. They say Kensington once locked a woman in one of the rooms, tried to force her to dig more rooms. But when she refused, he sent her to the surface with a bag of food and slammed the hatch shut behind her."

"We should be so lucky," Cece replied casually, though she found herself wondering if there was any truth to Curtis' words. She didn't fear the surface, but she did fear losing her work. And she *would* miss Greg—and even Curtis and his playful arguing.

"I'm serious," Curtis snapped. "They say it was even one of Kensington's own ancestors."

"No one would let him get away with that. Someone was just trying to scare you."

"Who would stop him? He's the Chief Director; no one would question him."

Sure, Cece thought, the Chief Director had the power to cast one of the four precious votes that could determine their future, but would the other Guardians really let her be thrown out? Did they fear Kensington's title that much? "What about the other officers? What about Greg and Lucia? Certainly they would stop him."

"Greg, sure. But ya know Lucia isn't going to cover for you if it's your fate that's being decided. Lucia and Kensington make two, so if you're lucky enough to get the public vote, the best you could get in council is a tie. Which means Kensington gets the decision. And you *know* he doesn't care about your work—or mine. No one does."

"Greg does."

"Only because he's the tech officer. He *has* to care." Curtis gave a sigh of defeat. "No one else cares, though. But at least they'll let us continue as long as we fill our shifts. So maybe you could just try to contribute a bit, ya know, so they don't throw you out and all your work ends up going to waste."

"Yeah. Maybe."

They entered into the lounge only moments later, and immediately Cece felt a wave of melancholy wash over her. It was the only true communal space they had at the Sanctuary, and currently it was filled near capacity. But even with the sixty or so bodies that occupied the space, the only sound that could be heard came from the holoset that projected from the north wall.

Currently, it displayed one of the few dozen shows that had happened to be saved to the device's hard drive when the Virus hit. Several half-circle rows of Guardians sat around it, many of them mouthing the words they had heard hundreds and hundreds of times before.

Cece instantly remembered why she avoided the place: a futile apathy permeated the room and threatened to poison her with its deathly stupor. Her parents sat in one corner, hands held as they lay sprawled on a couch watching a rerun of *I Married a Cyborg*. Kensington sat nearby, his robust form filling out one of the egg-shaped swivel-pods. The man's sixty-one years of living seemed to finally be taking its toll: the sparse collection of white hairs that clung to the sides of his head seemed thinner, his stubbled beard had fully lost its color, and even his large, round stomach was starting to sag. He spun in her direction, head tilting ever-so-slightly with curious interest.

Cece was about to turn around, already regretting taking up Curtis' invitation, when she saw Lucia and Greg sitting opposite the holoset. Greg waved her over; she waved back, gestured they'd be right over, then followed Curtis to the food station.

Jackson, one of the few other Guardians under twenty, was working that days shift behind the counter. "Hey, Curtis." He lifted a plate from a nearby stack, handed it to Curtis, then made a mark on a piece of paper attached to his clipboard.

Cece stepped up, and Kensington suddenly appeared in the lunch queue behind her.

"Well," he said, speaking in his lethargically slow tone, "it's been awhile since we've seen *you* around here."

"Yeah," Cece replied. "I've been working pretty hard lately."

"Hey, Cece," Jackson said flatly. He grabbed a plate, had it half way to her before he stopped suddenly. "Umm..."

Kensington sighed dramatically. "Well. . .what's the hold up, Jack?"

"She, um," Jackson stumbled, looked at his paper confused. "Cece doesn't have any portions."

"Hmm," Kensington intoned. "Well...doesn't look like you've been working *that* hard."

Jackson still held the plate half-extended. "Sir. What—what do I do?"

Kensington paused in thought. "Well... rules are

rules—if Cece doesn't show up for her shifts, then she hasn't earned the rewards." He focused his gaze onto Cece. "You can't just skip your work and use us as you see fit, ya know?"

"I'm not *skipping*—"

"You can just use one of my portions," Curtis interrupted.

Kensington flashed a menacing glare at Curtis.

Curtis shrunk back. "If that's okay with you, Mr. Kensignton. I just thought she could use the boost of energy so she can fill a shift later."

Kensington's head bobbed in contemplation as he looked Cece over, as though studying her. Eventually he gave a wide smile. "Well...I suppose. But only because I want you strong when we get you back to work. I'll expect to see your name on the list in the next day or two. Got it?"

"Yeah," Cece replied. "Sure."

"Good. Glad we understand each other. We were saved for a purpose, Cece, and it's important we don't get lazy."

It took every effort Cece had not to unleash the fury of contempt she held for Kensington. How dare *he* call *her* lazy! She stood motionless, trying to decide if she would let his hypocrisy pass unchecked.

Jackson thrust a plate in front of her, drawing her attention just enough to temper the anger that threatened to boil over.

She quickly filled her plate with beans, mash, and root vegetables, then hurried to a grab a chair across from Greg. Curtis fell into the seat next to her.

Cece sat silently, picking at her food as she tried to calm her thoughts.

"So," Greg began, "how's your android coming along?"

Cece sighed. "I'm having trouble getting it ready for a mind upload, but I'm thinking I just need to tweak a few more algorithms so it can operate without the parts I don't have."

Greg gave a heartfelt smile through his thick beard and tired eyes. "You'll get it soon, I'm sure. The fact that you've gotten this far is astound—"

Just then the bracelet around Cece's wrist burst into a series of loud, droning beeps that echoed through the room.

An uproar broke out amongst those watching the holoset, and several heads turned around wearing looks of disgust. A choir of "Shhh!" washed across the room.

Cece quickly fumbled at the device and clicked it off.

"New invention?" Greg asked after the deafening sound subsided. "What's this one do?"

Cece's eyes were wide. "It's my siren!" She paused in thought, startled by the implication.

Greg threw up his hands, confused. "For?"

"It's a motion detector," Cece said, excitement filling her tone more with each word. Then seeing the lack of understanding, she continued. "It's set to trigger only if the object in motion is emitting an electrical field..."

Greg stiffened, eyes narrowing. "On the surface?"

Cece smirked as she nodded.

"Kensington!" Greg shouted, using the table to push himself upright.

Cece eyes darkened as she shook her head, frantically mouthing "No! No! No!" as she gestured for him to quiet.

"Cece, this is too important."

Kensington spun in his chair, swallowed a bite of food. "Yes, Greg?"

"We've got trouble."

CHAPTER TWO

Kensington's approach had brought him to a stop between the ring of chairs and the dining tables, where Cece and Greg now stood opposite him. He was about to speak when Cece's mother appeared at his side, frustration weighing heavily on her features.

"What did my daughter do now?" she asked harshly.

Although Cece was only nineteen and her mother fifty-two, they could still easily pass as twins. They both shared the same walnut-hued eyes, the shoulder length coffee-brown hair that seemed to hide shadows within its thick folds, and both had oval faces with skin that radiated a warm, olive glow.

For Cece, staring at her mom was almost like looking in a mirror. If it wasn't for the bandana Cece kept her hair pulled under and the self-inflicted piercings in her ears and nose, the two would be easily confused. And although the resemblance was only physical, Cece worried that it somehow meant she would grow to become the unquestioning, fearful, and apathetic person her mother had become—or more likely, had always been.

"I detected a scrapper in the valley," Cece said proudly, "that's what I did. It could be an attack. Or maybe a wanderer? Either way, I think we should check it out."

The nearest Guardians seemed to awaken from their

slumber as they overheard the threat of danger, Cece's father included. He rose and joined his wife's side. He was a skinny man who lacked vitality, but even with gray hairs and a receding hairline he managed to maintain a baby face that spoke of naivety. "Greg," he said timidly, "Can you confirm this?"

"It's her instrument, not mine. But she knows what she's doing."

Scattered murmurings of fear began to spread through the throng.

Kensington cleared his throat, waving them into silence. "Easy. Easy." He turned his attention to Lucia. "Are you prepared to run a scouting mission?"

Lucia's well-built muscles tensed as she rose from her seat with a warrior's prowess, her thick black pony tail the only casual movement about her. She nodded, her bronzed features locking into a stern visage. "I'm always prepared," she growled, then turned to Greg. "Wanna come with?"

The mention of adventure seemed to awaken a dormant vibrancy from within Greg—the blue in his eyes brightened, his brown hair seemed to take on a glow, and even the heavy traces of red in his beard seemed more fiery. "Definitely," he said excitedly.

Lucia flashed a mischievous smile. "I'll grab the gear."

Cece thought of the power couple exploring without her, envied them for the time they were allowed to spend on the surface. Although they were nearly double her age, Cece felt a deep kinship with these two adults who actively pushed beyond their simple existence. Even if she didn't get along with Lucia, Cece respected the hard work the Chief of Security put in around the Sanctuary. And as Chief of Technology, Greg expanded his mind through endless hours of reading and tinkering. With so much in common, it only felt right she be at their side for *her* discovery.

Cece stopped Lucia before she could get away. "Wait! I'll come with you," Cece said. "I could use whatever extra gear you may have."

"You're not going anywhere," Cece's mom blurted before Lucia could reply. "If you think—"

"Laura," her father cut in, "calm down." Cece smiled at her father, surprised by his aid. Then she saw the look on his face turn guilty. "Listen, Cece. You can't go with them. It's too dangerous, and they don't need you out there anyway. Greg and Lucia have worked together a hundred times and you'd only get in the way."

Cece shrugged with defiance. "Well...I'm going anyway. What's the door code?"

Kensington laughed. "Good try. I know you haven't been around much, but that information is still only a privilege for the three officers."

"Then we can take a vote so it's less privileged," Cece demanded.

"We already took one when you—"

"Then we take another," Cece demanded. "Maybe people would feel differently now." She knew it was hopeless, but she couldn't stop the fight. She knew Curtis had been right: any vote she suggested would likely be shut down 3 to 1; and even if she managed to sway the public vote, a tie would still give Kensington the final decision as the Chief Director of the officers.

Lucia glanced impatiently at Kensington. "Talk some sense into her." She turned to Greg. "I'll be right back." And she was gone.

"Cece, your parents are right," Kensington said with a deep voice of authority. "Greg and Lucia, they know how to avoid the androids and make sure those machines don't find our bunker. They know how to avoid contamination. But you don't have that experience. You'd be risking everything we've fought so hard to protect." He shook his head as though confirming his own thoughts. "No, no. We can't let just anyone go up to the surface—not anymore."

"But if it wasn't for me—"

Kensington waved her to silence. "It's not up for discussion. It's too dangerous."

"Cece," her father pleaded, "don't make this hard on us. Just stay down here, where it's safe."

"It's safe on the surface," Cece replied. "You're just too afraid to find out for yourself. How do we know this scrapper is even hostile?"

"Because they all are," Kensington said matter-of-factly.

"We don't know that. We barely know anything since you won't let us explore the surface."

Her father's shoulders sagged in desperation. "Because we don't want you to get sick like your sister!"

"She *didn't* get sick from the Virus! When will you finally understand that? I was with her on the surface. I had the same—"

Her mother's eyes rimmed with moisture. "That's enough, Cece," she said, her tone verging on hysterical. "You're not going and that's the end of it."

Lucia returned then, two guns hanging by their straps over her shoulders and a gas mask in each hand. She tossed one to Greg. "Let's do it."

Cece looked at Greg with pleading eyes, but he only shrugged his defeat, the word "sorry" hanging unspoken on his lips. She made a point to glance at everyone else, shaking her head in disapproval of each. Not one of them, not even Curtis, were willing to come to her aid. "Next time I won't even tell you. Any of you." *Next time,* she thought, *I'll just go myself.*

She turned without another word and left, putting as much distance between herself and the infuriating Guardians as quickly as she could, yearning for the solace of her workshop and its sensible machinery.

*

Cece made her way through the halls with heavy strides, her muscles tense with frustration. Her mind reeled at the possibilities taking place above, on the surface, where she should be. It wasn't fair that Lucia and Greg got to go on *her* mission. She should have gone by herself when the alarm went off, should have lied and left the rest of the Guardians ignorant.

Why didn't I just go anyway? she wondered. *Because I didn't want Greg and Lucia to tell my parents, to tell Kensington? Because I knew they'd tell me to get lost?*

Why? Why did she feel the need to include them, to let them rule her?

She realized, to her own annoyance, that it was for their acceptance. She hated the notion, hated this inherent desire to belong. She cared little of what they thought about her, but for some reason she tip-toed around them, obeyed their rules in the hopes they might eventually accept her. That small glimmer of hope drove her to tolerate their rules, but her patience felt as though it was waning. She awoke each day filled with dread at the thought that one of the Guardians—save for Curtis or Greg—might come to her with more drama, more commands, more chastising.

She was torn: she felt happiest when left alone, when she had the peacefulness of solitude; but every dark night of sadness was rooted in her loneliness, in the haunting prospect of total isolation.

She wandered on, her mind in a tangle she could not unravel. Within this maze of thought she lost her awareness of destination, and soon found herself at the one place she avoided most in the Sanctuary: The Wall of the Lost.

A reminder of a time when she wasn't alone.

A reminder of a time when she had someone to confide in.

Dozens of pictures of the dead hung from the wall in rows, followed by just as many handwritten name tags that the Guardians had been forced to use after they had lost the ability to print photographs. And there, near the end of the collection, was the loss that was already rimming Cece's eyelids with tears.

Allison Schmidt. Age: 13.

Why had their parents waited so long to act? Why had they let Allison pass from the Earth when an alternative had existed? If only they hadn't locked Allison away when she was sick. If only they had let Cece act sooner, when Allison's mind had been strong enough to handle the stressful operation.

Cece recalled the door to the unused workshop that had been converted to a quarantine chamber. She recalled the look on Allison's face as it was pressed against the small window in the locked door, recalled Allison's soul piercing screams for help as her cheeks drowned in tears of fear and suffering.

The memory sent rivulets of tears down Cece's own cheeks, and the darkness of the deteriorated hallway seemed to close in on her.

She shook her head at the horrid reminder. *Why? Why?*

Why did they put such a depressing thing in a spot they all must pass every day? Why couldn't they put up pictures of their possibilities instead? Why not images of airplanes and space stations, of holograms and matter compilers, of endless fields of synthetic foods that could be altered to have any taste.

But no. They felt it necessary to drive home the sadness of their existence, to inspire fear with reminders of their losses.

Hello, World

Cece ripped down her sister's name tag. Allison was more than a name on a wall of negativity, she was a lifetime's worth of happy memories.

*

Cece wasted no time retrieving Allison's old camera once she returned to her room, eager for a reminder of better times. She collapsed onto her bed and began looking through the images.

The memory card was filled with pictures of their secret expeditions to the surface, of her and Allison standing atop the ruins of buildings, of them trying on every garment of clothing they had found in one of the nicer buildings in town. One picture even showed Cece's favorite green military jacket—bigger than she was at the time—that she still wore to this day, that she wore presently.

There were at least a hundred pictures Allison had taken that showed Cece toying with one of her many inventions. Cece laughed at herself, at how little had changed over the years.

Cece even came across an image of her old telescope—she was showing Allison how it worked; her sister's young face was beaming beneath the bright silver of the scope. Cece smiled at the memory and made a mental note to find the old telescope soon, to take it to the surface and gaze at the stars.

She continued through the images, pushing away the thoughts of the surface that only brought worry about Greg and Lucia. She soon came upon pictures of her parents, smiling wide as they celebrated Allison's birthday; which, judging by the homemade candles on the cake, had been her 12th.

Less than a year before her death.

Cece hesitated to continue through the photographs, knowing what was to come. She nearly put the camera away, but refused to miss a single memory of her sister. That was all she had—her memory. As she clicked through the images of Allison growing ever paler, ever skinnier, Cece's resentment of her parents only worsened. The time-stamp showed how long Allison had held on; but rather than think of her sister's strength, all Cece could think about was how long her parents had let Allison suffer. All of that pain could have been prevented if only her parents had had the courage to upload her consciousness.

The memories became overwhelming and she pushed the camera away. She covered her face with her pillow, and willed herself to sleep as she thought about what it would be like to have her sister back—in metal or flesh.

CHAPTER THREE

Cece had only just awoken when the knock came at her door the next morning. She stumbled sluggishly to her door and pushed it open.

One look at Greg's sorrow-filled face told her all she needed to know: nothing had been found.

"I know there was something out there," Cece told him. "I did a hundred tests with that stupid detector. Unless—somehow—a sheet of steel with active electronics got picked up and carried through the wind, there *was* something out there."

Greg shrugged, leaned against her desk. "Well if that's the case, it was quick and got well outta the valley before we got up there...because we searched everywhere."

"You couldn't have searched everywhere. The valley isn't that small."

Greg shot her a wry smirk. "You know what I mean," he replied flatly. "Now, we may give it another look tomorrow, but I think it's safe to assume that if anything was up there it's either long gone or hiding extremely well."

Cece accepted the misfortune, her shoulders slumping in defeat. She knew that Greg had nothing to gain by lying to her. If she could trust any Guardian, it was him. He had taught her everything he knew, and it was because of his lessons that she had fallen in love with technology and reading to begin with. He was the only other person who cared about the Sanctuary's technology as much as she did, although she had surpassed his understanding of it years earlier. "So...nothing? Nothing at all?"

"No tin-cans at least."

Cece's smile went wide. "But you did find something? Parts?"

Greg matched her grin as he swung the pack off his back and pulled out a book.

All of Cece's frustrations of the day instantly drained away with one look at the unknown book. She felt an overwhelming sense of joy at the prospect of a new story to lose herself in. She read the title: *Stranger in a Strange Land.*

"How do you always manage to find new things?" Cece asked with surprised awe. She knew she spent more time searching the valley than he did, yet he had an uncanny knack for turning up things she had somehow overlooked.

Greg handed her the book. "I've been doing this a long time, Cece."

"You don't want to read it first?"

"Nope. I figured I'd let you have the honors."

A sad smile of gratefulness tugged at Cece's features. The sudden change in mood drew her into a deep reflection, brought to her attention how much she appreciated having Greg in her life, how much it helped just to have one person who seemed to truly understand her.

Greg noticed her expression and rested a hand on her shoulder. "Hey. Are you alright?"

Cece nodded softly. "Yeah, it's just..." It was a lot of things—too many things. "Greg. Am I a bad person?"

Greg laughed. "Most definitely."

"No, seriously. I feel like I'm trying to do good here, learning as much as I can, trying to progress our technology—to make life better for everyone. But everyone treats me like I'm an enemy spy, like all of the stuff I do—the stuff I care about more than anything—is pointless and...evil."

She sighed. "The other day my dad told me that I didn't care about anyone but myself and my technology. And I think...I think he's nearly right. I don't like it here, Greg. I don't like the way people think, and I don't like the people."

Greg sat in thoughtful silence for several moments. "Can I tell you something, just between you and me?"

Cece nodded.

"I don't really like most people here either. They're not like you and me. They don't want to think, because that means being open to change. And change scares them. But the worlds a scary place, and sometimes it's hard to come to terms with the things we've learned. It's hard to know that once upon time we had billions of human beings and now we're down to hundreds. It's hard to know how primitive we are when only a few decades ago we were flying spaceships to the moon and other planets."

"And the worst part is," Greg continued, "is that every Guardian knows it was humans, our own kind, who spread the viruses that destroyed most of man and machine, and so they're afraid we could finish ourselves off if we learn what our ancestors knew. So can you really blame them for trying to keep things the same?"

"Yes. Because living in fear isn't going to make life any better; it's going to make it worse. We have to expand and learn—we have to get out of this hole."

"Facing your own fears is a hard kind of courage to find, Cece. You were lucky to have a sister who you could talk about things with. But most of us, most of us only had ourselves and our parents and the fear they taught us; and it's not easy to question the only things you know." He shook his head, trying to find the words. "All I'm saying is that you have to understand that not everyone has had the same upbringing as you, which means we probably won't agree on everything. But that's okay, because living together doesn't mean we have to like each other. All we need to do is respect each other."

"But they *don't* respect me. They try to make me into one of them. But I don't want to do the same thing everyday while I wait to die. I'd rather create and explore...so why can't they just let me do that?"

"Because they're afraid you'll upset the stability they've got going. Right now, most of us are happy just to get enough food and water to make it to the next day. And you know what, if they can't accept you for who you are, if they can't respect you...well, then that's their problem, and the best thing you can do is not let it bother you. Just keep doing what *you* love and try not to make too many waves that will unsettle their calm, comfortable waters."

"That's all I'm trying to do," Cece said, "but they won't let me."

"So maybe you should start doing it anyway. As long as you don't hurt anyone else, I think you should be free to do what you want."

Greg seemed to be struck by an idea then. He raised a finger, then gestured for the book back; Cece handed it to him. He retrieved a pen from his pocket and scribbled inside the cover.

"I'm not really sure how you've been doing it," he said while writing, "but don't worry about hiding your trips to the surface anymore. Just go. I'll fend off Kensington and Lucia and your parents. Just be careful, okay?—and hear them out when they have a concern. Eventually they'll stop trying to control you and just accept you for you." He paused. "My own parents didn't want me going to the surface. But I did anyway, and now look at me...I go up at least once a week. The important thing to remember is that your parents don't want you to go because they love you— not because they don't like you or what you do. They're simply afraid, Cece. But everyone has something they fear—even you."

"I'm just afraid of being a bad person."

"Other people are always going to try to make you feel like that so they can control you. But you get to choose whether or not you let their words affect you. You get to choose whether or not you're going to let that stop you from doing what makes you happy." He handed the book back to Cece.

Cece flipped it open, saw the seven digit passcode, and realized immediately what it would open. She gave a wide smile and wrapped her arms around his shoulders. "Thanks, Greg. For everything. I really needed this talk."

"You're welcome," he said, pulling back and looking her in the eyes. "Now just don't do anything stupid, okay?"

Cece laughed through the sadness. "Deal." She looked at the book still in her hands. "Hey... say I wanted to put this code to use now, would you mind covering for me while I go out? I think it'd really help to go read a bit and clear my mind."

"Do whatever makes you happy, Einstein."

"Einstein?"

"That's a conversation for another time. Now go on, get out of here and get some fresh air. But be careful."

"I always am."

"Liar."

CHAPTER FOUR

Cece took the long way around the Sanctuary, taking the branch through the living quarters so she wouldn't have to pass by the lounge.

She soon arrived outside the heavy, steel door that separated the Guardians from the outside world. Although it was nearly impenetrable, a simple seven digit code—which only the three officers were *supposed* to have—allowed easy passage. She brought her new book from her pack and tested Greg's inscription at the coded lock: *8 1 3 2 1 3 5*.

The door hissed as it unsealed, bringing a mischievous grin to Cece's features. She quickly slipped through, shut the door behind her, and made her way past the collection of tools, cargo, and gear that had barely seen any use since surface access was suspended for non-officers.

A short ladder climb up the silo-like tube and Cece found herself on the surface. She breathed in the outside air with an appreciative reverence. The fresh, crisp oxygen hinted at a vast quietness: a welcome liberation from the constricting, drama-filled Sanctuary.

It was bittersweet to think her people still feared such a beautiful world. She didn't doubt the Virus had happened—she'd seen the recordings left by her ancestors—but she believed the tiny infectious agent was long gone from the Earth, that it had died out with the host species it had so rapidly fed upon.

She didn't believe it was what had sickened and killed Allison either. Before her death, when the Guardians had still allowed limited access to the surface, the two of them had made almost every trip together, sharing everything, and Cece herself had never once felt sickened or infected.

She had never felt in danger of an android attack either.

But with that thought she suddenly remembered her motion detector's recent warning, and so she checked her bracelet to ensure it was still holding power; there was no reason to be careless. Besides, if an android appeared in the valley, she *wanted* to find it.

Cece let her mind return to the serenity of her peaceful surroundings. The silence was one of the biggest benefits of living in a dead world. Her mind embraced the calmness as she climbed over remnants of her ancestry, over the overgrown and broken roads filled with the rusted frames of cars and the brick-and-steel rubble that had fallen from deteriorated buildings. She found her way to the city's three-story capital building whose white marble exterior dripped with vines, as though they were fingers of the natural world attempting to reclaim the land by crushing the forgotten building within their grasp. She eyed the myriad of ladders the plants created with a secret nostalgia, then climbed their branches with a practiced grace.

Once she reached the top she settled into her usual perch overlooking the crumbling city. She could see the water tower in the distance that marked her home, could see the tell-tale signs of her people's instruments used to harvest the water and funnel it to their home below, the solar panels that lined the railing and draped the tower with electrical cords used to power her existence, and even the pitiful surface garden that had been so poorly tended.

She made a mental note to check up on her own hidden garden before she returned the Sanctuary; now that she was out of rations, she needed to make sure her own source of food was well cared for.

She wondered how many of her ancestors had passed by that exact tower before the Virus had stolen their lives, how many had thought it nothing more than a simple relic of an outdated generation. Had any of them known that there was a bunker below that housed the backup of every consciousness that had made the transformation from human to machine? Even then it had to have been important to keep such sensitive data and advanced technology secret from the masses, but surely the locals must have been curious why the primitive tower had been kept standing when they had the ability to fly in metal machines through space, to view each other through tablets across the world, to talk with their minds and live inside worlds made of only 1's and 0's yet unlimited in possibility.

She brought out her newest book from her pack—a relic of that mystical time—and admired the cover: the silhouette of man standing alone amidst an alien planet. Or at least she thought it was an alien planet...it could just as easily be Earth.

Every book she read made her feel like an explorer in an unknown world full of hidden mysteries, knowledge, and alien creatures. She yearned to have such a life for herself, but for now she would have to settle for imagining it, at least until her scout could confirm the alien parts of her own planet were safe.

Anxious to explore another new world, she began to read.

She was instantly lost within its pages as she followed the story about a man from Mars. She found herself grinning frequently as she read, her spirits lifted by the beauty of these dynamic characters who lived such interesting lives with flying cars and intrigue and even sex. It felt like she was there, in the world of the story, and all her frustrations with the Sanctuary subsided as she lost herself in the adventure of another existence. Hours fell away around her, while time passed more slowly inside her bubble of imagination.

When she finally raised her head again to face reality, she found the sun nearing the horizon and realized she had lost all track of time.

A gentle breeze blew by and cooled the warmth the sun had imparted on her skin. Her eyes fluttered closed as she embraced the euphoric sensation and lost herself in contentment.

She turned her head suddenly, thinking she had heard a sound in the distance. Was it an android? She quieted her breath and tilted her head ever so slightly toward the noise: waiting, listening.

Nothing.

A scratching sound—a scurrying. Something was moving nearby, and fast.

Then she saw it: an emaciated cat running across the edge of a decrepit building almost two blocks away. Filled with excitement by the prospect of a new friend, she quickly shifted into a stealthy crouch.

Cece gathered her belongings, vaulted over the edge of the building with a grace only gained by confidence and years of muscle memory, then slid in short spurts down the curving limbs to the ground below. She trembled with anxiety. Although it was believed most animals had proved immune to the Virus, she had found they rarely came into the valley; she didn't want to lose this chance to nurse the creature to health, and maybe even gain a much-needed companion in the process.

She stayed low to the ground and moved in short, quiet steps as she covered the distance to the building the cat pranced upon. Brick by brick Cece climbed, using a drainage pipe as a consistent counterpoint to the loose stones she was grasping at with her opposite hand. Her hand soon came down heavily atop the ledge of the three story building and she yanked herself upward.

The stone in her hand gave way, sending large chunks

of the wall soaring past her. Her left hand slipped down the pipe as she reached out for a new handhold. Her right hand swung and found the hole left behind by the broken masonry.

She dangled thirty feet in the air, her right hand the only thing keeping her from a fall that would crush her against the jumble of steel and concrete below.

Her mind flashed with the image of her body laying crippled in the cold, dark night, not a single Guardian who knew where she was.

Her breaths were coming in quick deep spurts now. She strengthened her grip, kicked violently against the building, and scrambled upward. She lifted her chest over the ledge, then threw her legs over the rim.

She lay frozen in fatigue, dirt clinging to the sweaty coating on her skin. Her stomach rose and fell in quick, heavy breaths of relief and adrenaline as her mind raced with the consequences she had so barely avoided.

Then a new sound came, unlike any a cat could make. It was a beep—subtle, yet intricate. Electronic.

Panic struck her; this must be what her sensor had picked up, what Greg and Lucia had been unable to find. She glanced at her bracelet, saw the screen scratched and broken—likely the result of her near-fall. She would have to use her own senses to find the source.

She rolled onto her stomach, crawled to the building's edge where she waited for the sound to return to guide her eyes. It did, and she traced its echo back to a set of communal-living apartments.

She knew her people had already searched the place for any useful remnants, so whatever this was, it was new. She watched the cluster of buildings for minute after tense minute, wondering if an android might emerge at any given moment.

But as darkness filled the sky and lengthened the shadows around her, the beep continued to drone on with with zero movement to accompany it—zero variation of any kind, be it tone, echo, or location.

Encouraged by curiosity, she slid down the pipe that had saved her half an hour before and made her way toward the sound. She climbed a short set of stairs and entered an overgrown courtyard where the grasses rose into a thicket, filling the area like the tight but chaotic patterns on a circuit board. To her sides, at the edge of the courtyard, were brick arches that delineated each apartment's entrance from the next.

When the beep came again, Cece lost all sense of destination. The sound seemed to come from everywhere, and it took her several moments to realize it was an echo. She sighed with frustration at the uncooperative acoustics, then set to encircling the walkway that ran along the interior archways, listening for where the echo was the loudest.

But after two laps she was none the wiser and ready to give up. She stood still, thinking, the beep echoing in her mind every so often, taunting her. Even if it was an echo, it should still get louder if—

Wait a second, she thought.

She cautiously made her way into the dense grasses, heading toward the center of the courtyard. The beep sounded again, this time noticeably louder. She silently reprimanded herself for not being intelligent enough to have figured out the puzzle sooner. She followed the noise until she found herself at the edge of a well, and the next beep confirmed her success.

She peered over the edge to see a jumble of broken clockwork and metals heaped at the bottom. With the last glints of daylight, she was able to make out shreds of artificial skin and a human face that stuck out at the end of a metallic spine.

"Now what would you be doing all the way out here?" she said, feeling herself be overtaken by a thrilling curiosity.

But her growing elation dissolved as realization

struck: her first run in with an android and it was shattered to pieces—unable to talk, unable to share, unable to teach her anything at all.

Then she noticed a black box—*a hard-drive perhaps?*—that was unlike any she had seen before, and surrounding it was an abundance of high-quality engineering materials. A broken android, Cece decided, didn't mean a useless android.

She broke off in a sprint toward the water tower. When she arrived at the double doors that hid the cellar below, she flipped open the inner hatch, placed her feet and hands on the side of the steel ladder, then slid the twenty feet down to where the entrance to the Sanctuary waited. Instead of going in, she retrieved the rope and hook the Guardians had used in the past to move goods between surface and bunker. After glancing at the sky above, she also decided to grab a rechargeable flashlight from the nearby pile of tools.

Back at the well, she realized the black box in the center of the android's chest was the source of the beep that had tormented her; in her mind, that signified importance, and thus made it her priority. She took aim and tossed the tied-off hook toward it.

After nearly an hour of fishing in the dim glow of her flashlight, she managed to hook the box and pull it into her waiting hands. She contemplated fishing for more parts, but with the sun gone and the body being too heavy to lift by herself, she decided to return home. She tossed the box into her backpack and returned to the Sanctuary, only to realize just before going in that the beep, a sound she had zoned out after hearing it so often, would give away her discovery.

She retrieved a meager collection of tools from just outside the Sanctuary door—an adjustable wrench, pliers, and a screwdriver with interchangeable heads—and set to work on disabling the speaker that continually emitted the conspicuous noise. She ripped off the cover, then popped off the speaker that rested on the beacon's circuit board.

"Well it's about goddamn time," Greg's voice said from behind.

Cece jumped, startled. "Greg. Shit. You scared the hell out of me."

Greg stood in the open, steel entrance to the Sanctuary. "*I* scared *you?* Damnit, Cece, do you know how long you've been gone? I thought for sure you ran into some scrapper who had his way with you. What the hell have you been doing?"

"I—there was a cat."

He opened his mouth with a planned fury, then stopped suddenly, laughing away his tension. "A cat?" he asked, incredulous. "All of this worry over a *cat?*"

"Yes," Cece lied. "All this worry over a cat."

Greg's eyes narrowed and he stepped closer. "Yeah. Then what's that?" He nodded at the box with the disabled beacon resting in her hands.

"Just a drive I found. Might have some information I can use. Or at the least could be some extra memory."

"And you weren't planning on checking it in, huh?"

"I—I mean, I don't think there's anything to worry about."

Greg returned a harshly disapproving glare. "Damnit, Cece. Going to the surface is one thing, but you can't bring unscanned tech in here. If that thing is infected it could destroy every single consciousness in the database—and the memories that go with them."

"I was going to scan it myself."

"Yeah—once it was already within our system. I'm trying to cover for you and you do shit like this?"

Cece felt like she had just been shot in the stomach. "I—you told me to do what I wanted. That so long as I wasn't hurting anybody I should do what—"

"But this *could* hurt people, Cece. You running around and tinkering—that's fine, but I can't let you bring that in here unchecked. I just can't. If you want to keep it, you have to do an official scan."

"Greg. Please, don't make me do this. The last thing I need is for anyone else to know I went out. Everyone's already upset with me as is."

Greg sighed, stroked his beard in thought. "I can scan it for you," he said, "then give it to you after. How's that?"

"But what if it has something on it Kensington doesn't like and he wants to take it from me?"

"What could it possibly—"

"Please," Cece interrupted. "Just let me have this one." A moment lingered. "I promise, I'll scan it myself on an isolated terminal. It will never touch our network."

"You're putting me in a shitty situation here, you know that, right?"

"I know, and I'm sorry. But you know I'm only trying to do right by everybody. I'm trying to help us. Just like you taught me."

Greg couldn't hold back his smile as he shook his head. "You know, I'm going to have to learn how to say no to you one day."

Cece smiled. "Hopefully not anytime soon."

CHAPTER FIVE

Cece went straight to her bedroom, locked away the newly-acquired hard drive in the old wooden desk that sat at her bedside, then fell face first onto the bed.

She yearned to explore the contents of her new, precious device, but fatigue hung too heavy. Her body hurt all over thanks to the day's abundance of activity—which, most draining of all, included the near-catastrophic fall from the rooftop that had left her with a myriad of scrapes and bruised muscles. The mere thought of having to sit at attention at her work desk sounded like too painful an effort.

And after the dramatic emotions stirred awake in dealing with her fellow Guardians the night before, and the fluctuations of fear and hope caused by the presence of the broken android, her mind was equally as debilitated.

The last thing she wanted to do was risk damaging the device because her mind was too exhausted to avoid stupid mistakes. She needed to wind down the night with something that required less thinking, less risk.

She rolled across her bed to retrieve the book from her pack, then reversed the movement to settle into a cozy reading position against her pillow.

A welcoming peace of mind enveloped her as soon as she flipped the book open.

After nearly an hour of reading she had made it within a hundred pages of finishing the book. Every part of her wanted to continue, but her exhaustion was too great. She put down the book, switched off her light, and thought how dearly she owed Greg for the amazing story. It was unlike anything she had read before. While it had less technology than many of the others, which she would have expected to be disappointed by, it had something else she had never seen so deeply explored and questioned—sex.

It was one of the three things the Guardians used to define their lives, its priority lower than the upkeep of the database and equal with watching holovision. And since the database had been designed as a fail-safe that could run indefinitely with as little upkeep as possible, sex was the go-to activity when not sitting in front of the holoset. It also had the added benefit of reproduction, which offered the perfect way for her people to indulge and pass the time, while still feeling like they were doing the work fate had saved them for.

It was often the topic of choice as everyone attempted to figure out who was sleeping with whom. And whenever a couple showed signs of attraction, everyone conspired to coax them into having as much sex as possible. The Guardians needed people more than ever in the Sanctuary, and a child born of love was the best way to ensure a stable future.

Cece, however, had no desire for a child, nor had she ever had sex.

Her chastity was no secret, and was likely another reason the Guardians resented her, another reason they thought she was strange. It wasn't a lack of interest that kept her innocent, though; she yearned for the experience, yearned to experience everything.

Sure, every male within her age range had made the offer at least once, but she had quickly turned them down. Some had been more persistent than others, like Curtis, but most had given up after the first try or two.

She had seen the power sex had over the Guardians, and feared that she would succumb to it the same way her people had. She had seen the powerful bond sex had forced between people who only brought each other down, who had nothing in common except their willingness to overlook their chemistry in order to dedicate themselves to this time-passing pleasure that made them forget they live in a cage. They accepted their limited lives and abusive relationships with a numbed complacency, and didn't care as long as they had sex.

She couldn't let that happen to her. She didn't want to stay in her cage, and she didn't want to lie to herself like that, to feel like she needed someone in her life to complete her—especially if the sex wasn't rooted in love.

Even then, the idea of investing so much of herself in another person terrified her. What if she lost them, like she had lost her sister? She never wanted such an excruciating pain again—a pain that had yet to subside. Besides, what future could they have? Cece had no plans of sticking around the Sanctuary—all her work was meant to get her beyond the valley as quickly and safely as possible; she would have left already if she had more information that indicated she could survive. But when that time came, when her android was complete, she couldn't think of a single Guardian who would go with her...

...save for maybe Greg or Curtis.

While Greg was an undeniably handsome man, he wasn't an option; he was more of a father figure to Cece than the man who had actually brought her into the world. So that left Curtis.

She had thought about it before, had thought about it often. Curtis was intelligent enough, and he seemed to understand her, which *was* what she wanted in a lover: understanding. But she couldn't let sex become an excuse, couldn't let it stop her from getting away when she was so close. And she couldn't risk falling for him, only to lose him when she left. So instead, she sated the urge herself and kept others at bay, and saved that precious gift for a day when she had established a life she could be satisfied with.

But she needed a release now, something to unravel the tension that racked her body.

She fell asleep a short while later, her mind blank and her body still tingling.

CHAPTER SIX

While the rest of the Guardians slept, Cece worked furiously at her terminal, fueled by the knowledge that the information stored on her new drive could forever alter the future of her species and their place on Earth.

She had awoken in the dead hours of the night, stirred by some nightmare she couldn't recall. She had attempted to return to the grasp of sleep, but her thoughts had drifted to the hard drive and she became too curious to quiet her mind. So she had connected the drive to her local terminal and was dealt a profound discovery—one which, four hours later, was still pumping adrenaline throughout her body.

Hundreds of thousands of files were loaded onto the drive, suggesting a level of technology far more advanced than that of most scraps they found around the town. Such a large capacity for storage was unheard of. Not even the few androids past Guardians had managed to scrap had more than negligibly small drives for their long-term memory.

Thanks to Greg's guidance and her immersion into the Sanctuary's user manuals, she knew that the first android models—the only models that had made it to production before the Virus struck—had been designed so that most of their long-term memory wasn't stored on the android itself, but rather transmitted through the air to and from the Central Hub: a database located at Singularity Industries' headquarters.

In addition to the long-term memories, the Hub stored all of humankind's history, knowledge, and any possible skills the android might want to access at any given moment. Apparently Cece's ancestors had been so advanced that they had mastered the art of instantaneously sending great amounts of data from their computers through the air, and this approach was far more efficient and dynamic than focusing on physical, on-board storage. This left the androids with only three small drives for memory: one each for sensory, short-term, and long-term memory. This android's drive, however, was monstrous, verging on thousands of times more storage than the common on-board memory.

Greg had said that *Singularity Industries* were their only ancestors who had access to such technology, and that they had only used it in two places: the Central Hub and the Sanctuary. But the Sanctuary used their drives for the database of souls, which made them unusable for anything else. The Central Hub's collection was said to have been destroyed when news of the Virus had spread and the riots broke out. It was that destruction of the Central Hub that had rendered every android, from that point forward, void of any knowledge, skills, or memories—save for those they had stored in their meager on-board drives.

It pained Cece to think about. She couldn't imagine the sense of loss that afflicted those brave souls who had been the pioneers of evolution. They had embraced godhood—the ability to know any skill or knowledge without years of study, to perform any hobby without a constant fear of damage to their weak flesh—only to lose it all, only to become impotent and short-sighted and inferior to their original form.

That loss still paled in comparison to the blow dealt to humanity: the destruction of the only existing compendium of all human knowledge and technology.

But this drive—this drive said otherwise. It said something that Greg and the user manuals had not.

It said there was *another* place that used such technology—that a third, equally as hidden, equally as technologically-advanced bunker existed. While her Sanctuary acted as a backup for the consciousnesses of the humans who made the transition, this *other* place appeared to be a database backup for the memories and skill-sets of the androids—and most importantly, for the compendium of all human knowledge they had drawn from to give them their godlike intelligence.

It was the embodiment of everything Cece wanted from life, and part of it was now in her possession.

She was astounded she had never hypothesized the existence of another backup before. It was simultaneously the most inspiring and demoralizing of realizations. And though her mind had never entertained the idea before, it seemed so obvious now. If her people were charged to protect the consciousness aspect of the Central Hub, then of course there would be another bunker to protect the other half of the androids' critical functioning.

Now staring at the hundreds of thousands of files on the drive, she had no idea where to begin. She scrolled past "Ancient Cultures," past "American Revolution," past "Assassinations(Presidential)," and onto "Astrophysics."

Astrophysics, she reflected with enthralling wonderment. *The science of space.* What endless things she could do with this information! She could learn forever—and this was only the beginning.

She scanned through the files, making note of future topics she wanted to obsess over. She started making backups onto her personal terminal of her favorites; after reading her newest book, many of those files had to do with Aliens. She wished she could copy it all, but even if they rounded up every spare drive they had, it wouldn't come close to holding this much data. Anything *that* large was already backing-up human consciousnesses.

After hours of scanning the "A's" on the drive, she decided to do a reverse-sort to see how far into the alphabet the drive went. The top file wasn't a folder, though; it was a .*lnk* file entitled "Beacon." She opened the file to find a huge string of numbers which, guessing from the file name, was most likely the code used to access the beacon that had originally led her to the drive. She quickly wrote down the code in case she needed it later. The next several files were .GLD files, a file-type she had never seen before. She highlighted the top bulk of files, copied them onto her personal terminal, then attempted to open them.

Nothing.

She tried again several times only to fail each attempt.

She hacked at it for nearly an hour, testing each file with a variety of programs. She tried to read them as source code, as text, as an image, as a virtual model—none of them worked. She returned to the drive, scanning through more of the files in the hope of finding some clue.

She reached the last folder "Evangelicalism," and, dejected, gave a heavy sigh. She didn't like being ignorant of the secrets on this most miraculous of devices. She wanted to know everything about it.

And then she saw it. The file just above "Evangelicalism" wasn't like the rest; it was an executable.

With renewed hope, she ran the .exe file from the drive. It brought up a new interface, with one simple button that read: "Load Geographical Location Data."

GLD, she realized with a triumphant smile. She clicked the button and selected all of her copied GLD files. Dozens of maps exploded onto the screen, each overlaid by a longitude and latitude grid. Several thick red lines traced arcing paths across the geography while the image of a satellite rotated on the screen, and the word "Triangulating" flashed across the top of her monitor. The on-screen maps began to zoom inward, one square at a time and at increasingly smaller factors.

When it finally stopped, Cece's breathing did as well. She stared dumbfounded at the screen. She knew the valley she lived in so well that there was no mistaking it.

There was no mistaking the water tower that looked like a simple circle on the map, surrounded by the greenery of their garden. *It can't be,* she thought, as she dragged a box around the tower. The terminal zoomed in closer and she could see the solar panels and strands of wires her people had run into their hatch below. She could see the crumbling debris she had climbed through a hundred times. This wasn't a picture from the past, she realized, but a live image.

With an anxious haste and sweaty palms, she manipulated the image to zoom out. A red circle appeared around her valley once the view had retreated far enough. It was labeled "Soul Sanctuary: Brain Backup," and next to it was a string of coordinates.

A single red line ran northeast from her valley and off the edge of the screen. She followed it, moving the screen several pans across the geographical landscape, past live images of mountain peaks and thick forest, all the way to the coast where she found herself looking at another red circle: "Central Hub: CPU," with coordinates. Another red line extended northwest from there. She zoomed out and followed this new line until she found herself looking at the most beautiful thing she had ever seen: "Alexandria: CPU Backup," with accompanying coordinates.

She zoomed in on Alexandria and discovered another small valley with a water tower. The town looked deserted, the water tower undisturbed.

A simple yet profound epiphany struck: if she placed this drive inside her android, then it would have all the information it needed to find the other bunker and retrieve the full collection of hard drives. Her android could find that precious store of all human knowledge and bring it back to her people.

It would rocket her people to levels of which she had always dreamed of. It could be the very thing that would allow them to ensure the Virus was gone from the planet, or even make technology to cure it—or at least prevent it.

It would give her blueprints to create planes that could fly through the sky, satellite cameras that would let her see anywhere in the world—like what she stared at now—and an endless number of other inventions she could use to bring humanity back to the magnificent culture it had once been.

All she needed to do was finish her android. If she could only—*wait. The android in the well,* she thought suddenly. It would have any part she could possibly need. Certainly with its parts she could complete the mechanical body she had spent the past years building.

She shut down her terminal, locked the drive in her desk, and threw on her military jacket. As she exited her room, Curtis came strolling down the hall towards her.

Not now, she thought. There was no reason for Curtis to be in this part of the Sanctuary unless he intended to see her. She hesitated; she couldn't let him know about her tunnel; she would have to use the *real* entrance.

Curtis stopped at her approach, but Cece continued past.

Curtis' steps shuffled quickly behind. "And where are you off to in such a rush?"

Cece consider lying, then thought of Greg's advice: *do what you want as long as you don't hurt anyone.* "Outside," she replied curtly.

Curtis caught up, attempted to slow her. "And how are you going to do that without the code?"

"I know the code."

"Good joke. But what are you *really* doing?"

"I'm going outside," Cece said without slowing her pace. "I know where to find the scrapper that I detected yesterday, and I'm going to go harvest some parts from it."

Curtis hesitated in thought. "Wait. Are you serious? Did it show up on your detector again? How do you know it's dead?"

"Listen," Cece said. "I'm in a hurry. So come with me or don't."

Curtis talked on, but Cece paid him little attention. All she could think about was getting the parts she needed to get her android on its way to Alexandria, to the backup of all human knowledge.

"What now?" Curtis asked when they arrived at the locked door that separated the Guardians from the outside world.

Cece stepped forward, punched in Greg's code: *8 1 3 2 1 3 5.*

The door whispered open.

"How—" Curtis uttered from behind.

Cece retrieved the rope and hook she had used the day before and made her way up the ladder.

"Cece," Curtis said, chasing her up the ladder. "I'm not sure this is a good idea. What if Kensington finds out?"

"Don't tell him and he won't."

"I'm not going to, but there was a reason he put an end to surface trips."

"Allison didn't have the Virus," Cece replied sternly as she emerged onto the surface. She continued on to the courtyard apartments where the well and her future awaited; Curtis followed closely behind.

"Do you have any idea where you're going?" he asked as they walked through the deserted streets.

Cece had to give him credit: he had put aside his fears of Kensington and the Virus and stuck with her; maybe she could trust him after all. "Yes. I've done this a hundred times."

Curtis laughed, then suddenly cut short when he realized she wasn't joking. "You're serious, aren't you?"

"Very serious. Now keep up. The scrapper is just up here."

They entered into the courtyard and Cece blazed through the tall grass with determination. She dropped the rope at the edge and looped the rope around the pulley-bar that ran above the well. She looked down to gauge her approach, and her high of discovery came crashing down.

Curtis noted her dispirited shock and appeared at her side, glancing down into the well. "I don't see it."

Neither did Cece.

It was gone. Somehow, it was gone.

"It was here," Cece pleaded. "I know it was here." And then she saw them: the sunken, rigid footprints of an android heading away from the well.

"If you wanted to get me outside alone, all you had to do was say so," Curtis said, moving closer. He said it teasingly, but Cece caught the hints of truth in his tone.

Cece pointed at the tracks in the dirt. "Look at the tracks, Curtis. Do they look human to you?"

"Hmm," Curtis murmured, "good point. They're probably just old tracks though."

"They're not," Cece replied definitively as she studied the footprints.

"It is quite nice out here, though, isn't it? Maybe we should come out here again soon...maybe grab some food from the garden? Just me and you—and we can even just talk about our inventions, so you wouldn't feel like you were wasting your time."

Cece was flattered, but it wasn't the time. Her mind was on other things, like the fact that there were two trails: one that led into the town and another that came in from the northwest. She tried to recall the scene from the day before, attempting to remember if anything had been different. Her memory was sharp, but not enough to remember something that had seemed so trivial. *I should have paid better attention yesterday,* she told herself. Her curiosity was her gift and she had failed to utilize it.

She saw her own footprints and found herself imagining what it would be like to have metal feet. She tried to imagine how, if she were an android walking through the desolate town, she would come to make such a path. What was the circumstance that led to the android falling into the well? She had been so excited at her find before that she hadn't stopped to ask how this intelligent machine could have simply stumbled down into a walled hole.

She looked back at her and Curtis' footprints, then back at the android's. Her eyes narrowed suddenly as she noticed an obvious clue: two tracks came to the well but only one walked away. It was all there in the dirt, the story told by the imprints of pointy metal toes.

"Cece," Curtis pleaded. "Can't you listen to me for five seconds? I'm trying to ask you out for a date."

Cece's mind was in overdrive, and Curtis' plea passed through the air without comprehension. The android hadn't been alone. So what had happened? Had they fought and one pushed the other into the well? The footprints showed no signs of struggle. If there were two, where had the other been when she first heard the beacon on the drive? Maybe it had come after, looking for his friend who had somehow, stupidly, managed to fall into the well? Maybe one was hunting the other?

But why would two androids be fighting? What could—

The hard drive. Of course. Any android would be so lucky, and if one knew another had it...She understood how strong the desire for knowledge could be; surely an android would kill for such a wealth of information and storage space. Her curiosity subsided suddenly, and in its wake came a wave of fear. One android was still out there, heading towards the town, looking for, and possibly killing for, her new drive.

Curtis stood watching her, defeated. "Yes, Curtis," he said in a high-pitched, mimicking tone. "That sounds great. I would love to have a picnic with you. Thanks for thinking of me enough to invite me. And thanks for even noting how much I love talking about my work and appreciating that as well."

"We've gotta get out of here," Cece said, surprised by the trepidation in her voice.

"What's your deal?" Curtis asked. "It's impossible to talk to you anymore. You're either too busy or you ignore everything I say—that anyone says."

"Curtis, I'm sorry, but now is not—"

"It's never a good time," Curtis erupted in frustration. "Every moment is so dedicated to your work that there is never a good time. And I know how it is, Cece. I do. I know what it's like to care so deeply about something that people don't understand, to have a passion that others think is a pointless pursuit. That's why we have to stick together. Because you're one of the only people who understands me, and I think I'm probably one of the only people who can understand you. So could you at least pretend you give half a damn about me?"

Silence.

Cece had never considered how bad things were for him, how lonely he likely felt. The depth of her own loneliness had been the reason she had become so invested in her work, but she had only needed that form of escapism for the past four years or so; Allison had been there to talk to and share secrets with for the years before that. She could only imagine how hard it's been on Curtis having had no one this whole time—no siblings or parents or friends who understood him. "Curtis, I...I never thought—Why didn't you say something? Why didn't you tell me how you felt before?"

Curtis threw his arms up, head shaking, expression aghast. "I have. I mean, I've tried—hundreds of times I've tried. But it's so impossible to get through to you; you shut everyone out. And I can't blame you for the most part, but I thought one day you might actually see how similar the two of us are, and maybe—just maybe—give me a chance."

"Curtis, I never meant—"

A thunderclap sounded suddenly, followed by the clatter of crashing bricks. Chunks of stone and mortar flew in every direction. Cece slammed her eyes shut instinctively as she turned away from the flying debris. A hot slash of pain struck across her cheek and nose. Curtis threw his arm around her and they slammed into the ground together. Cece glanced back at the well where bits of broken brick crumbled to the ground. She turned to where her survival instincts told her the sound—which she now realized was a gunshot—had come from.

An android was bounding across the rooftops toward them, one arm raised with a weapon in hand. His armor glimmered in the sun, and marked on his chest was an emblem that appeared to be an "M" inside an embellished circle. Cece decided this android was more than typical.

She turned to Curtis who was shaking violently. "Stay low and follow me."

She led him through the thick grass of the courtyard, out the front entrance, across the street and into a decrepit building.

"What do we do?" Curtis stammered, panting. "What do we do?"

"Just stick with me," Cece told him. She led them up a set of winding stairs where she stopped to peer out a window. The android was making his way across the street toward their building. Panic began to take root in her gut. "Come on!" she yelled to Curtis.

They sprinted across the second-story hallway and jumped through a window onto an adjoining rooftop. Still running, they leaped across a three foot gap onto a nearby building and continued on until they came to its edge.

"Jump," Cece commanded, gasping.

Curtis looked at her, incredulous. "No way."

It was a fifteen foot drop, and their only option. Cece heard the echo of metal feet on the stairs behind them. "Just roll forward when you connect with the ground. Like this."

Cece leaped to the ground, curled into a ball as she landed and somersaulted forward. She looked back at Curtis who still stood terrified at the ledge.

"I can't do it," he told her.

"Do it or you die." Her words were void of judgment and emotion. It was the simple truth, and Curtis realized it. He took several deep breaths so heavy that each nearly bent him into a bow...then he went for it. He landed awkwardly, causing his knees to buckle beneath him and sending his body crashing hard against the ground.

Cece rushed to his side and lifted him up. "Can you walk?"

Curtis let out a pain-filled moan as he rose, then nodded. The two of them stumbled another block across the city and into the government building. The place was a maze, but Cece had been inside it a hundred times and knew every turn by heart. She got them to the top floor, three stories high, then leaned over a railing that looked down into the lobby. The android came rushing in and she made a point to let it see them. Once she knew she had its attention, she took them through a series of hallways to a well-hidden stairwell that led to the roof—to her reading perch. They ran to the edge, and she turned to Curtis with a serious look that said *this isn't up for argument.* "Just hold on and follow my lead. The vines will hold."

Curtis looked at the thirty foot drop and shook his head. "There's no way. I can't. I—I can't"

"We have to." Cece vaulted over the edge with ease and began to descend. Curtis slowly brought one leg over the ledge and froze for several moments as he looked for a hold.

"Just let your feet slide down the branches," Cece called up to him as she blazed downward, already only a few feet from the ground. "It will hold. Let your hands guide you."

She bounced anxiously as she waited on the ground, adrenaline making it impossible to hold still as she watched him struggle. Curtis double and triple-checked each hold, moving with a grating hesitance until his feet finally found soil. Cece immediately took him by the arm and pulled him into a sprint toward the water tower. Cece led them behind a building in case they hadn't lost the android yet, in case it happened to be watching their movements.

They finally made it to the tower, dropped into the hatch, slid down the ladder, and landed with a crash on the steel flooring. Cece quickly punched in the passcode, and together they rushed through the entrance into the Sanctuary, slamming the door shut behind them as their bodies collapsed against it in exhaustion.

CHAPTER SEVEN

"What do we do?" Curtis asked, sweat dripping from his face, body lurching from panicked breaths.

Cece looked at the broken bracelet on her wrist and regretted not having fixed it right away. "We get to the sensor in my workshop and see if that thing sticks around in the valley."

Curtis wasn't fond of the decision, and began complaining as soon as they set off for Cece's workshop. He wanted to go straight to their parents, to warn them. "We're all dead if that thing comes down here," he said over and over, pleading: "We need their help."

But the last thing Cece needed was more undue attention from the so-called 'adults'. If they found out she had brought in scrapper parts without scanning them, if they found out she had been sneaking outside, they would...they would...

Her thoughts went to Curtis' rumor, to Kensington's threat. Would they really throw her out? Would they take force against her if she kept sneaking out and avoiding shifts? She had always viewed the Guardians as meek, but if they actually rallied against her there would be nothing she could do to stop them.

They entered into the workshop, and Cece felt the bulk of her tension subside at the silence of her sensors. Had the android left the valley so quickly? She worried her detector could be malfunctioning, but it seemed like it had worked before and she saw no reason to question the good fortune.

Now feeling secure, Curtis took the moment to draw attention to the blood dripping from Cece's face, commenting that she "should probably do something about that." They decided to go back to Cece's room where she could treat the wound in a clean—and most importantly, private—place.

"I'm sorry, by the way," Cece said as they made their way to her room. "About—about how I've treated you. I never knew that was how you felt, and I just... I just really got caught up in my work. When Allison..." She took a deep breath. "Ever since we lost her, my—my work was the only way I could stop crying. And so I immersed myself in it as much as I could, and I guess...I guess ever since then it just kind of became a habit. So...I guess I just wanted to say thanks for drawing it to my attention." Cece hated the way her words sounded, so broken and feeble.

"It's okay," Curtis said, his tone warm and sympathetic. "I should have said something sooner. I think I was just too nervous." He looked at her with a roguish smile. "You're intimidating, Cece. You know that, right?"

She returned his smile. "I never meant to be. You were great out there, by the way. For not knowing the terrain, you were impressive."

"Did I just hear a compliment from Cecilia Schmidt? I think my ears were damaged by those gunshots."

She gave him a playful push. They're eyes met, and she realized how much she was enjoying having Curtis around. He wasn't feeble and unquestioning like everyone else. He challenged her, something no one else did—at least not intellectually. "So is that invitation for the picnic still open—once the outside is safe and all?"

His face lit up. "Of course."

They continued to her room enveloped in a comfortable silence. Cece's quietness was a result of the nervousness she felt in her gut, and the struggles of her mind trying to understand why it was that Curtis' presence seemed to cause it. It was an unfamiliar sensation—confusing and scary, but exciting. She wondered if Curtis' quietness was a sign that his head was swimming with the same possibilities.

When Cece opened the door to her room, every tingly emotion she felt was blasted away in an inferno of betrayal-fueled anger. Her bed hung off its frame and was littered with her papers and electronic gadgetry; her personal notes and research had been mixed and thrown around with carelessness; and her desk was pulled away from the wall, the drawers hanging limply open—including the one where her newest hard drive had been hidden away.

She shook her head with teeth clenched, heavy breaths forcing out through her nose. She could only manage to mutter "Greg" before she broke into an angry stride out of the room.

Curtis followed, asking a stream of confused questions. Although she wanted to explain everything, she could only think about the possible consequences that lay ahead, of the irrevocable shift in one of her most valued relationships, of the sickening hurt of Greg's betrayal.

When they arrived at Greg's door, Cece banged so furiously against it that she wondered halfway through the assault if she might have broken her hand.

Curtis placed a hand on her shoulder and attempted to calm her. His attempts were in vain though, as Cece continued her rampage. But no matter how unrelenting her attack the door remained closed, and so she wasted no time heading to the lounge.

Curtis called out for her to wait, but she ran on, navigating the tight hallways as fast as she could.

Arriving out of breath at the lounge, she saw the ever-familiar gathering of her judges: her parents, Kensington, Greg and Lucia. Their eyes went wide when they saw her standing in the opening, her body quivering with impotent rage and her face still dripping with blood.

Greg was the first to rise, concerned. "Cece, what the hell happened?"

"Where is it?" Cece demanded.

"Now wait a second," Greg told her, gesturing for her to calm down. "Let me explain."

"Explain what? How you destroyed my stuff? How you stole my property?" Cece stepped forward, looking Greg straight in the eyes. "How you betrayed me!"

"That was me," Lucia said proudly as she came to Greg's aid. "He told me what you did. And unlike him, I'm not going to risk everything we're protecting here just so you could keep your new toy."

Curtis entered the lounge then, exhausted.

Kensington approached Cece, ignoring Curtis' entrance. "There is a reason we don't allow such dangerous things to be brought into the Sanctuary without our approval, young lady. Why can every else seem to figure it out except for you? When are you going to learn there are rules here?" He shook his head, irritation dominating his features. "Thanks to you—" He poked a finger toward Cece, "—the database could have gotten a virus. And now we have to change the entry code so you don't get us all killed with your carelessness. And just in case you think you can figure out the next one, I'll make sure it will only let you out, not in."

Her mother came next with confused, sad eyes. "What—what happened to your face?" Her features filled with shadow. "You were just outside *again*, weren't you? Weren't you?"

"Of course she was, Laura," Kensington said. "How do you think—"

"I took her out," Curtis said, making his presence known. "It's my fault. I told her I wanted to investigate, to see if I could find any parts for my work."

Kensington shook his head disapprovingly. "Just wait 'till I talk to your parents, Curtis. How disappointed they'll be to hear Cece has tainted you with her toxic attitude."

Cece glanced back at Curtis and shook her head. "No, he's just trying to cover for me. It was me. I wanted to get the parts for myself and I made him go."

"You two brought back more unscanned electronics, didn't you?" Kensington prodded angrily. "Be honest with us now. You've already done enough damage as is."

"Damage?" Curtis asked, incredulous. "She's probably the only one trying to fix this broken place. If it wasn't for her sensor, we wouldn't even have known there's an android wandering around our valley right now."

Cece's eyes went wide and she gestured silence to Curtis.

"An android," Kensington repeated stupidly. "In the town? Right now?"

Cece glanced at Greg, disgusted. She recalled his words with a hint of spite—recalled how she didn't need to care about people who only brought her down. How, so long as she wasn't hurting anyone else, she should be free to do as she chose. "Yes. I'm sure. That's how I got this," she said, drawing a line through the blood on her cheek. "And it's likely here for my drive—the one you stole from me."

"Should we give it back?" Cece's mother asked, her tone dripping with fear.

"No!" Cece erupted. "We can't. It holds more information about our past than we could learn in a lifetime. If the droid comes looking for it, we must protect it with everything we have. It's our only chance for a future!"

"We won't have a future if he kills us," Kensington said. "Greg, is the drive in a place we can easily retrieve it if we need? We may have to quickly rid ourselves of it if she brought trouble our way."

Greg flinched, suddenly torn. "Now hold on. If she's right about what's on that drive, then she may have a point."

"Some pointless information on a drive isn't worth

58

the thousands of minds we were fated to protect. We can't—"

"You weren't fated to do anything," Cece cut in. "We're nothing but the descendants of some lucky technicians who managed to get their families to the bunker before they were infected." She paused: the calm in the storm. "And another thing, why do you even care about those *minds* you so vehemently protect? The only thing those *minds* represent are the people who made the choice to become the very things that now walk the surface—the very machines you hate and fear. And aside from Curtis, none of you are even trying to give these minds a body. So guess where they're likely going, if anywhere?" She waited for a response, and when none came she roared, "into androids!" She looked at them with a disgusted disapproval, her tone turning futile. "Humanity deserved to be left with better than the likes of you." She turned to Greg, stared him down. "If you have any honor, any courage or wisdom, you'll keep that drive safe. Otherwise, you've damned our entire species."

CHAPTER EIGHT

"How dare they!" Cece yelled as she threw her bed back onto its frame. The struggle of shifting the awkward bed back into place sent another surge of anger through her. Her room was a place of solace, a place she was free to be herself, and to see it so disrespected infuriated her to no end. She was thankful Curtis had understood her need to be alone; she needed be able to vent without an audience.

And vent she did, muttering curses under her breath as she angrily gathered her scattered papers, fixed the broken drawers hanging from the desk where the hard drive had been stored, and brought some general sense of organization back to her home.

She fell onto the bed once her room was back in an acceptable state. She became exhausted as the adrenaline drained from her body, though her mind continued creating an endless stream of strategies for getting her hard drive back.

A knock came to the door, then it immediately swung open. Kensington's figure stood outlined in the doorway.

Cece felt bile rise in her throat. The weight of his presence washed away every tiny ounce of peacefulness she had gained since last seeing him. His interruption of her much needed solitude inflamed her. "I don't have anything else in here. You should know that after you destroyed all my stuff in your search."

Kensington closed the door behind him, moved to

stand over her—to talk down to her. "You forced us into action, Cece. We don't take pleasure in fighting with you, but we have to have some form of order."

"Your *order* will be the death of humanity. Your *order* isn't helping anything. Your *order* gets fat watching HV, and the only time you do anything else is when you stop me from trying to make things better."

"Well...*what's better*... is what's best for everyone, not just you. And what's best for everyone is order. What's best is when everyone contributes and doesn't risk what we have struggled so hard to maintain. And you're not contributing, though you are risking everything. And I think it's about time that comes to an end."

"What are you going to put an end to? My questions, or my answers? Which is it that bothers you so deeply? That I question your order, or that I've found the answers that show how pointless your order really is."

"You've shown nothing other than that you're a selfish little girl who only cares about herself. You've been with no man, which gives us no population growth; you've not worked a shift, which gives us no food or a better lifestyle; you've snuck out consistently—oh yes, I know about your trips to the surface—which only endangers our divine purpose in protecting those minds and their memories. You give us nothing, and you risk everything."

"You want me to give you sex, food, and submission to your lies, yet I'm the selfish one? You don't ask me to contribute, you ask me to be a slave. But humanity doesn't need slaves, it needs thinkers and creators. Not fat old men who are too lazy to give life the effort it deserves."

She shook her head at him solemnly, then continued. "But I'm tired of being your slave. This is not *your* Sanctuary. You don't get to lay claim to my life because your daddy was the Director. That doesn't make you any more important than me or anything I do. That doesn't give you control over me."

Kensington gave her a malicious smile. "You don't

CHAPTER NINE

The Sanctuary was not the largest of places, and obviously not built with its current usage in mind. The history passed down by word of mouth and computer data made it clear that the bunker had been built to be self-sufficient, had been designed to sustain a team of fifty employees indefinitely. This served two purposes: it prevented the employees from the need to leave the Sanctuary—possibly drawing undue attention from the townsfolk—and also kept them safe, so they could continue to maintain the database even if tragedy struck the region. It was this design in infrastructure that had allowed the Guardians to survive as long as they had, though it did little to ease the struggle of the one hundred twenty-three Guardians who currently resided there.

Aside from the room Cece had claimed—where the Kernal stood like a sentinel stoically waiting to copy consciousnesses from mind to machine—two other workshops existed, and each had been separated into living quarters. There was also the laboratory Curtis occupied, which hadn't required much modification from its original layout in order to accommodate his practice of synthetic biology. There was the lounge that acted as the only communal space and also doubled as the kitchen. Then there was the restricted room—the crown jewel—where the database of souls hid behind a thick steel door. Lastly, there were the barracks: a honeycomb of rooms that housed the residents of the Sanctuary and which continually expanded as the Guardians dug through the earth to make space for a population that was growing at a dangerously slow pace.

Since Kensington's visit, it was at these dirt walls that Cece spent every other morning, fulfilling the servitude her people had forced upon her by throwing shovel after shovel of earth to make space for future residents.

The work was mind-numbing; it required no thought and gave no sense of accomplishment. Every moment spent digging made Cece feel like she was living a lie, made her feel as dirty as she looked after each shift, as though her mind and body could sense the deviation from her purpose in life. It only took a week for her to be completely drained by the effort of forcing herself through the meaningless work that left her feeling unfulfilled. It was fatiguing to maintain a positive mind in the face of such an obvious sacrifice of self. Her ability to think was severely dulled after each exhausting shift, and she began to understand why the Guardians numbed their nights with HV and sex and food: because their minds were too emptied to be used for anything but lazy pleasure.

She might have fallen into that same apathetic spiral those first days if not for Curtis. He had been her rock, had allowed her to cry in his arms as she suffered to cope with being condemned to routine numbness, of losing her passion thanks to the threat of exile. And since she refused to go to the lounge, refused to mingle with the very people who had sided with Kensington to decide her life for her, she would have been forced to succumb to the melancholy of complete alienation without him.

But Curtis pushed her, kept her focused. On the days where she didn't lay exhausted in his arms, she worked feverishly at inventions she hoped would allow her to secure the safety of her stolen drive. Curtis often stuck around to lend a hand, even brought some of his own equipment to her workshop so they didn't feel alone as they worked on their personal projects. It surprised Cece how much she enjoyed his company, how much better she worked and felt when she had someone to talk to—even if it was just a random piece of conversation in between soldering circuits, running through equations, or writing computer code.

Cece spent those intitial work sessions ensuring her drive wouldn't leave the compound. The first thing she built was an additional sensor: a simple motion detector that would monitor the hatch to the outside world. Curtis had covered for her while she had used the secret tunnel to put it into place. If anyone went outside she would be there, ready to make sure her drive wasn't with them. She built a new bracelet receiver for it as well, and integrated her old android sensor to it so she only needed the one device.

This new ability to track the movements around her small world—a world where it felt as though everyone was against her—filled her with a sense of power and control. She kept the device around her wrist at all times as a reminder that her intelligence—her ingenuity, drive, and passion—was her advantage. The Guardians were encultured with unquestioning apathy, and that made them weak where she would be strong.

When her surveillance equipment was finished, she had turned her attention to searching. But even as small as the Sanctuary was, it had taken Cece four days of panicked exploration to search every inch of it—at least everywhere she could gain access to. She had even performed stealth missions to break into and investigate Greg and Lucia's rooms for any sign of the drive's location.

But she had come up empty, no closer than when she had started. The only place she hadn't searched was behind the impenetrable door that protected the database. And while that would be the most secure place to hide the drive, it didn't seem likely that Kensington—with his fear of computer viruses—would place the questionable device next to the database he so vehemently defended.

That left two options: the drive was either destroyed, or Greg had done a damn good job of hiding it. The only thing that kept Cece from crumbling apart in despair was the knowledge that Greg—regardless of the betrayal—shared her deep reverence for technology and understood the implications of the drive. After all, it was his guidance that had endowed Cece with a passion for learning. If anyone in the Sanctuary could appreciate the contents of the drive besides herself, it would be him.

After a week of working and searching, Cece was no closer to finding her drive. She was, however, closer to Curtis—much closer. They shared a common struggle, and their outcast status meant nothing when they were together. And with the amount of time they spent in the comfort of each others' arms, their friendship quickly became more than that.

They couldn't pursue it, though; Cece wouldn't allow it.

Not yet.

There was too much going on—too much she needed to do—and the last thing she needed was to cloud her mind with distracting thoughts of romance and the confusion that came with it. And what if they became intimate and Curtis suddenly no longer wanted to be with her. She needed him now more than ever, and it was better that he be a friend rather than nothing at all.

Curtis had respected Cece's need to keep him from getting too close for nearly two weeks; but now, back in Cece's room after a long day of engineering, his desire was finally getting the better of him.

"Would it really be so bad if we took things to another level?" he asked, sitting at the desk that had once guarded the drive. "The teasing is starting to become torture."

Cece lay sprawled out on her bed, eyes closed with fatigue. "Yes. I've seen what relationships do to people. Greg hasn't been the same since Lucia dragged him into her bed. I can't lose my focus like he did. Not right now. "

"But we're not them. We actually have stuff in common. We actually like each other."

"Which would likely make it even worse. You know that once we start I'm going to keep thinking about you, keep wanting you. It's just how the brain works. And until I get my drive back and the android out and on its way, I...I just think we should hold off."

Curtis slouched over with a sigh, and then, as if gaining a shot of adrenaline, rose straight up and clapped his hands together. Cece roused from her reverie and saw him standing above her brandishing a devious grin.

"Okay, then," he said excitedly. "No more sensors or prevention crap. It's time to go on the offensive. We're going to figure out how to get you back that drive, and we're doing it now."

Cece laughed. She was surprised by how foreign the emotion felt to her in that moment, but was even more taken by how good it felt. "Well now I know how to get you motivated."

"Guilty," he admitted with a smile. "Okay. So, what do we know?"

"I appreciate what you're trying to do, but I really don't want to do this right now," Cece said. She gave a moan of exhaustion, closed her eyes. "I just want to not think for awhile."

"Well the sooner we figure this out, the sooner you can stop thinking, and the sooner we can—well, you know."

"Now I'm not so sure I want to find it."

"You'll pay for those words." A wad of paper struck Cece in the face.

Cece shot upright. "Hey! Careful. These are important," she said as she straightened out the paper.

Curtis scanned over the papers as he shuffled through them. "I don't know. That one looked like it was just scribbles." He examined another page. "And this one is just random numbers." He looked up at her. "I'm starting to wonder if you actually make anything or if you just write a lot of junk on paper and pretend it's science. That's what you do, isn't it? You've been pretending this whole time. Now I understand why you're so intimidated by me..."

Cece got up, refusing to let the challenge to her intelligence pass unchecked. She looked at the design on the first paper. "*That* is a weapon I've been working on so that my android can defend itself. It harnesses the electricity in the body to emit an EMP outwards."

Curtis nodded. "Okay, okay. I don't believe you, but impressive. And this?"

Cece looked at the string of numbers. "*That* is simply the result of a calculation. And that," she pointed at the numbers below it, "that–" She froze as her mind exploded in a frenzy of understanding.

Curtis cut in, noticing her hesitance. "It's just scribbles, isn't it? I knew it."

Cece recalled the file in which that number had been stored in, recalled that the file had resided with the location files.

Her head fell back in dumbfounded shame and carried her body with it back onto the bed, where she proceeded to silently berate herself for her stupidity. She had been so concerned about making sure the drive stayed in the Sanctuary, so determined she could find it the old fashioned way, that she had completely forgotten about the beacon that had originally drawn her to the drive.

She *had* disabled its wailing siren before bringing it into the Sanctuary, but that had only silenced it; there was no reason it shouldn't still be emitting a signal—a signal that she could track; a signal whose access code was written down on the paper in Curtis' hand.

Every bit of the day's fatigue dissipated instantly as a plan formulated in her mind. She jumped up and kissed Curtis on the cheek.

"You are amazing," she told him. "Thank you."

Curtis beamed. "Well thank you. You're amazing too." He wrapped his arms around her and attempted to pull her closer.

Cece pulled away, shook her head. "Nope. Now you've gotta leave."

Curtis' features blanked immediately. "You're kidding..."

"Nope. I've got work to do and I won't be able to think it through with you around."

"But we've been working together for almost two weeks now."

"But I knew what I was doing then. I didn't have to invent something new. Now I do." Cece saw the hurt splayed across his face. "I'm sorry. I promise I'll find you as soon as I figure it out."

CHAPTER TEN

Cece struggled to focus as she sifted through half a dozen years' worth of accumulated notes and the files she had copied from the hard drive. Her mind was too noisy to concentrate as she continually wondered if she had gone too far by kicking Curtis out. Maybe it *would have* been better to let him stay; at least then her guilt wouldn't be dominating her thoughts.

The design for her tracking device was coming together though, even if it was slow. The problem, she had quickly realized, was not the difficulty of making it work, but rather the resources required. The only logical design she could come up with required pieces of tech that were in short supply.

She needed an antenna, which would require dismantling the sensor that watched the outside world for androids. But even then, the Sanctuary lacked any technology that could access outside networks, and without such parts she wouldn't be able to make the antenna's transmission powerful enough to link to the beacon's satellite. That meant she would have to make her invention portable so she could carry it like a dowsing rod.

She put together a list of all the components she would need and set to searching through her workshop. The bulk of items she found easily enough, but it soon became obvious she was short on a few crucial pieces: a screen and memory chip, both of which couldn't consume too much power since it would have to be portable.

Cece knew exactly where to get both, but the idea broke her heart. Her sister's camera was one of her most prized possessions, and the thought of tearing it apart felt wrong, inconceivable. Then again, this was the future of humanity in question. Without that drive, her android wouldn't have a destination. Without that drive, humankind would likely lose thousands of years of technological advancements. She decided that her sister, who had lived more fully than most other humans, would have understood.

With painful effort, Cece moved all of the images she could onto her personal terminal. The image files were large though, taking up titanic amounts of memory compared to the text files...and she still had over fifty images left to copy when her computer warned that it was out of memory. Having already filtered through and deleted her own personal files to make space for the ones from the drive, she was left with another gut-wrenching choice: delete the pictures, or the folders full of the human knowledge she may never be able to get back.

She decided quicker than she expected, and dozens of folders soon faded out of existence: memories of love were worth the loss of knowledge.

After reconciling her grief at the loss, she prepared for a quick trip to the surface to dismantle her sensor for the parts she needed. But when she thought about being forced to use her tunnel because of Kensington's threat to change the entrance passcode, she decided now would be as good a time as any to solve another problem that had been weighing on her.

Kensington and Lucia had proved they had the ability to uncover her secrets, and the thought of them finding and blocking her access to her hidden tunnel terrified her; and so she had spent the last two weeks, during her down time between projects, working on a new creation that would ensure they couldn't trap her—couldn't hold her prisoner—inside the Sanctuary.

She retrieved the chip from her workbench that signified that freedom. It had one simple purpose: to reset the operating system it was connected to by draining the device of its memory. To trigger it, all she would have to do is give it the proper seven digit input: 0 0 0 0 0 1 0. But it was a one-time-use trick, for after the system it was connected to had reset itself, her chip wouldn't be recognized—would be deemed incompatible and thus rejected.

With her chip and a backpack full of tools, Cece made the trip through her tunnel, across the surface, and up the side of the water tower, where she set to work on her prime task of disassembling her sensor.

Once she had salvaged the parts she needed, she worked her way to the hatch below and down the ladder to the Sanctuary's secure entryway.

She approached the keypad and attempted the code Greg had given her: *8 1 3 2 1 3 5*.

The door remain closed; Cece cursed Kensington under her breath.

She retrieved her tools from her pack and removed the faceplate that rested over the keypad. Once she isolated the proper wires that would carry the data from her chip into the lock, she brought out her chip and quickly attached it to the security system, then restored the faceplate to its proper place.

Since she couldn't test the single-use trick, all she could do now was hope that it worked when the time came.

She gathered up her tools, made sure her parts were safely packed away, then returned to her workshop the same way she had left.

With a new peace of mind and all the components she needed, she went to her room and set about the heart-wrenching activity of breaking down Allison's antique camera.

After that, the night fell into a haze of programming

and engineering, soldering and calculating, testing and debugging. When she finally finished, the clock told her the sun was rising outside. Although every part of her yearned to put the tracker to use right away, to test it and go searching for the drive, she knew she needed to stick to her and Curtis' more subtle plan.

CHAPTER ELEVEN

Cece and Curtis pretended to be as casual as possible as they wandered through the halls. It was the perfect disguise, as everyone seemed to believe the young romance had completely robbed Cece of her concern for the drive they had stolen from her.

Cece could imagine the rumors: "They've been spending so much time together," and, "Oh, to be young and in love," and probably most commonly, "It's about time." But the Guardians were blinded by their desires, by their lust to have everyone fit inside a box they could understand; they didn't see the camera-shaped tracking device she held concealed between her and Curtis' huddled bodies.

She glanced at it every few moments, reading the primitive yet powerful display. It was a simple radar design with two dots being tracked on the screen: hers in the middle as the source, and the hard drives rotating around them as the destination. She kept them heading toward the blinking signal of the hard drive, which several times led them bumping into walls and dead-ends. Within the confines of the small Sanctuary, it didn't take long before they found themselves closing in on the hard drive's signal. To her great amazement it took them toward the database of souls, the one place she was almost certain it wouldn't be.

They reached the high-security door, and Cece stared at her tracker with confusion. "It says we've still got quite a ways to go. It looks as though it's northeast more, beyond the database."

"Could you have messed up the programming?" Curtis asked. "It might just be off calibration a bit. You did make it in a night..."

Cece stared at him with cold eyes.

"You *can* make mistakes, you know."

"I really only made a channel, though—an interface to read out what was made by people way smarter than me. And I checked my code over a dozen times. If this thing says it's farther down, it's farther down."

"Any farther is a dead end," Curtis said.

Hallways branched off to each side: one led toward the lounge, the other toward the living quarters. The hard drive's dot seemed to lie along the way to the living quarters, though much too close to be in any actual room. With no other option, they followed the hall that led to the barracks.

They passed the dot as they made their way, its location shown inside the wall on their left between them and database—a wall that consisted of several feet of thick concrete, stone, and packed earth.

It has to be with the database, Cece thought over and over as they continued, stopping only when the living quarters came into sight. Since leaving the front door of the vault that housed the database they had walked almost two hundred feet, and still the dot blinked to their left.

Confusion tore at Cece; the geometry simply didn't make sense. If her tracking device was operating correctly, the hard drive was *not* with the database, but not quite in the living quarters either.

They continued on until they reached the first door in the living quarters; it was one Cece knew well. She knocked on Greg's door, and prepared to berate him with every bit of guilt she could muster. She had run into him twice since he had stolen the drive, and could tell he truly felt bad for siding against her. *As he should,* Cece thought as she continued to bang on the door.

The door remained closed, which was even better for Cece. Having successfully broken in once before, she was confident she could do it again. This time, however, she wouldn't fail in her search. She tested the lock with a heavy twist at the knob and the door unexpectedly gave way. A sense of weightlessness struck her as she began to fall, and a split-second choice appeared in her mind: drop the tracker or accept the impact.

She decided to take the fall.

Curtis reached out, caught her before the impact came, and lifted her back onto her feet. Cece flashed him a thankful smile when she recovered her senses and continued in as though nothing had happened.

"Wait," Curtis called to her. "What if Greg comes back?"

"What if he does?" Cece asked with a devious grin. Curtis sighed, reluctantly stepped inside after her, and closed the door.

Cece followed the tracker until she came face to face with the back wall of Greg's room, where a small assortment of clothes hung on a rack. The radar, however, still showed a noticeable distance between her dot and that of the drive. She turned to Curtis, astounded. "I think it's in the wall...between us and the vault."

She ripped the clothes from the rack and tossed them aside, revealing a wall of cardboard boxes. She turned to Curtis. "Can you go through these while I search the wall?"

"I'm not sure I feel comfortable going through his stuff..."

Cece threw up her hands. "But it's what we came here to do."

"I didn't know we'd be going through anyone's stuff."

"I'll go through it if you don't, and then we'll just have to be here longer."

Curtis slumped in defeat. "Fine." He went to his

knees in front of the boxes and began sliding them out of the makeshift closet with quick, yet careful movements. Cece followed his progress, sliding her hands across the spaces he exposed, feeling for any grooves that might reveal some sort of passageway. Every bit of her focus was on her touch and the wall in front of her; she wanted every mental faculty she had working to solve the riddle. When Curtis faltered at her side, she knew he had found something.

"Cece," Curtis called out with whispered excitement.

She was already there, eyes pleading for him to give up his newly found secret. Curtis embraced a bravado of showmanship, reached for the next row of boxes, grabbed the sides to move them back, then gave a gentle yank to showcase their adhesion to the wall.

Cece felt ripples of hope cascade through her. She rushed to Curtis' opposite side and began shaking the boxes. The first three columns held firm, but the fourth and the fifth collapsed to the ground. She gestured for Curtis to follow her lead as she gripped the unmoving boxes, and together they yanked forcefully.

The boxes held resolute.

"Sideways," Cece commanded, tilting her head toward the right wall. Curtis nodded, and together they brought their strength to bear. But the boxes only bent. Cece nodded left, then pulled toward herself while Curtis pushed. Nothing.

Cece immediately fell back in defeat, but Curtis continued pushing. Without Cece's arms pulling on the boxes, the wall shifted suddenly and slid backward several inches, tracking along a rail that appeared on the ceiling.

They paused, shared a grin of victory, then both pushed against the wall with all their weight. It slid straight back a few feet, then trailed off to the side, coming to rest inside an alcove. A hallway that looked identical to the rest within the Sanctuary laid out a long path ahead of them, and the pair wasted no time making their way down the hidden passage.

Cece glanced at the tracker with a gleeful smile as they went. "It should be just up around this corner," she said.

They entered into a small room that appeared to be a storage area. A mixture of hurt and anger swelled inside Cece as she studied the contents of the shelves that lined the walls. They were filled to overflowing with books she had never read before and heaps of electronics that looked far more advanced than any of the technology she had ever had access to within the Sanctuary. If even half of this room had been available in the past years, she could have easily finished her android by now—and probably a dozen of other innovations that could have bettered her life and that of her people. Yet it was all here, hidden away in secret.

"Do you see it?" Curtis asked, seemingly oblivious to the gravity of the situation.

Cece forced her roiling thoughts of betrayal into a dark corner of her mind and returned her gaze to the tracker. She zoomed the screen closer and it rendered the hard drive's dot a mere few feet ahead of her. She walked forward, eyes scanning the room of squandered goods until she came to a stop in front of a sleek silver box bound by a simple latch. With anxious fingers she worked the latch free and the cover lifted effortlessly to reveal her drive. She retrieved it with a quick swipe, embraced it into a hug, eyes falling closed as if cherishing the return of an old friend.

"Can we leave now?" Curtis asked, a nervous tremor in his tone.

"Soon." Cece wasn't ready to leave behind so many promising tools of creation—especially the books...they were a priority. The mechanical and electrical components were nice, but substitutes could always be found, and such pieces were worthless without an understanding of their usage. But knowledge...knowledge could coalesce to form infinite possibilities, infinite ripples of creation. Knowledge was the hand that wielded the tool, and no tool could ever reach its potential without a competent hand.

And the stories...they often taught her just as much—if not more—than the user manuals and guidebooks.

She scanned through the books, wondering which might transport her to a beautiful world of fantasy and science, or perhaps provide her with a wealth of information she could either use herself or program into her android. She loaded her arms with books: one by Einstein—who she recalled Greg mentioning; one by Philip K Dick—which she was immediately attracted to when she saw the word Android in the title of one of his stories; and another by Nietzsche that sounded like an interesting read. More books fell atop the pile, including survivor manuals and books on integrating nano-tech and neuroscience, on quantum-computing and quantum-physics, on astrophysics and machine fabrication.

Her arms bowed, but she wasn't done. Next she went through the gadgetry. She quickly realized she wanted too much, emptied a nearby box, then began to load it with her goods. The books at the bottom of the box soon became covered by an abundance of carbon nanotubes, nano-injectors and packages full of unprogrammed nanobots, by servos and brackets and braces and chassis, by glass marked as "unbreakable" and heaps of circuit boards, memory drives and chips that each rivaled the cutting-edge technology of the hard drive she had fought so dearly to be clutching once more.

Once Cece's appetite was sated, they made their way from the secret room, sneaking through the halls with an overflowing box hoisted in each of their arms.

They were back in Cece's room barely an hour after having first set out with the tracker. They had done their best to return Greg's room back to its original state before they had left, but it would likely only pass as undisturbed in casual observance. But Cece couldn't care less; she now had all the resources she needed to finish her android and get it on its way—everything except a consciousness.

She hoped the ancient scanner on the Kernal would still work properly after so many years of disuse, hoped her body and mind were stronger than her sister's had been.

She hoped *she* could survive the upload.

CHAPTER TWELVE

More than forty eight hours had passed since breaking into Greg's room, and still he had yet to confront Cece. The lack of his appearance worried her more than his presence would have. He was a smart man, and she was certain he would have discovered their poorly covered tracks by now. So why hadn't he said something?

She pushed the worry from her mind. The last two days had been too good to let her mind dwell on unknowns. Using her newly acquired parts and guidebooks, she had discovered what breakthrough fixes she needed to make in order to complete her android. Now all she had to do was put in the hard work, then her dream would come to fruition.

The following days proved the greatest of Cece's entire life. Even with the mornings of digging at the wall to keep Kensington off her back, she spent hours each day bent over her workbench, shifting between mechanical and software work. Each minor success chipped away at her fear that one of the Guardians would come to punish her for her delinquent behavior, but eventually nothing existed to her outside of the workshop...save for Curtis' visits and food deliveries. He showed a great deal of patience with her as she worked, respecting her devotion to the fulfillment of her dream.

Cece soon realized her appreciation of Curtis had left the seedling stage and had grown into an intimacy-bearing tree on the verge of blooming. His presence had acted as an anchor to her frenzied level of production, providing her with regular doses of human interaction that recharged her mind and made her work easier to focus on than ever before. So after six days, when the time came to put all of her hard work to the test, she made sure she wasn't alone.

With Curtis at her side to share in the glorious moment, she had watched the android run through to completion, coalescing its 57,316 files and processes into a functioning—yet unthinking—machine. And while the on-screen analysis had shown green across the board for critical functions, three hundred files had corrupted or failed to initialize properly. They were minor issues mostly: a loss of some of the more subtle senses of touch, as well as the finer points of taste and smell.

Although those minor issues were big losses in their own right, they seemed almost non-existent compared to the scale of the failures in neurotransmitter functionality. While the serotonin and melatonin modules had succeeded, the dopamine simulator had riddled the machine with bugs. Dopamine algorithms were still firing, just not consistently. Curtis had joked it made the machine more like her that way anyway: void of consistent emotion and riddled with logic. Curtis quickly realized Cece hadn't seen the humor in the joke, and with the added stress of uploading her mind adding an edge to her attitude, he had decided it was best to leave her alone for awhile.

That had been nearly two hours ago, though, and since then she had run through the checklist in the Kernal's user-manual at least a dozen times in preparation to upload her consciousness. She had to make sure every component was operational and showed no signs of possible failure, since her brain would be the first the machine would process since her sister's, with almost a hundred years since the one before that. But if she succeeded, her consciousness would be stored into the database of souls, forever saving a copy of her mind as it presently existed; more importantly, it would be transferable to her android.

The thought was invigorating: an exact machine-replica of her entire mind might soon roam the planet, gathering knowledge of the outside world and eventually bringing her back the drives that would give her endless amounts of knowledge to study and learn from. She could think of nothing better than the ability to learn forever, with the understanding that anything she learned—anything she could envision—could eventually become a reality. That was the promise of her ancestors, to turn imagination into creation. With those drives, she would pick up where they had left off.

"What if this thing wakes up and just decides it doesn't want to get the drives?" Curtis had asked. She had explained that she was way ahead of him, had already programmed in a prime directive to guide the android. She had given the machine a set of priorities, leaving survival as the only thing more important to the android than retrieving the drive. Collection of other technology—especially if it improved the android itself—was also a high priority. It would be her treasure hunter; it would be what she couldn't be, live the life she couldn't.

Now on her seventh read-through of the user manual, she let her mind wander to the magical possibilities her ancestor's knowledge of technology could perform. She felt like a magician in one of her fantasies, breathing life into the dead, sending souls through time and space. While half of her mind reeled in fantastical thoughts, the other half ran through mathematical equations, through if-then statements and what ifs. The noise of possibility was a cacophony inside her head, but all around her was a globe of silence... until a voice pierced the bubble.

"Well...that's not something I like to see you reading," Greg said as he approached, his tone carrying a playful edge.

Cece's head shot upright in panic. Had Greg finally

discovered his secret room had been plundered? She studied his face, ran through every emotional-recognition technique she had learned from years of AI programming, but his blank features gave no hint as to the purpose of the visit.

"You would think it would be required reading for every Guardian," Cece replied. "Then again, I guess there are some things you leaders don't want us knowing about." She flashed him a taunting smile.

Greg's stoic facade evaporated. "Sometimes it's better that way. Sometimes ignorance *is* better."

Cece cringed. "I'm afraid I must disagree with you there."

He approached with a sad smile and took up a familiar position leaning on a crate across from Cece's workbench. "Cece... you can' t really plan to go through with this. It's not worth it."

"Not worth it?" Cece asked, incredulous. "What could be *more* worth it?"

"Use a different consciousness—any besides your own. We have thousands. Why does it have to be *your* mind? It doesn't benefit you at all to have your mind in that machine instead of someone else's."

"But it does—because I'll know it's me out there enjoying the adventure. Once I upload my mind, this machine will be just like me. It will have my memories to build on, my mind that it will use to experience pleasure. It will make decisions based on what I would do. In nearly every way it will be as if it was me out there. And when it comes back, I can review its mind and see how such a journey would have affected me."

"But it still won't be *you*," Greg said pointedly. "How could you be so rational in everything else you do, only to risk your life just so you can pretend that it matters what mind is inside that body—just so you can fool yourself into believing that there is some benefit to *you*. You get nothing from it, Cece. Nothing. No memories. No experience. No knowledge or adventure. You're risking your life for absolutely nothing. All I've taught you and all the hope you bring to humanity—gone, because you want to act like a child and give yourself this self-indulgent, egotistical fantasy."

She opened her mouth to answer, but no words came to her. She wanted to argue, to defend her logic against his, but he had made his point well. *Why did it have to be me?* she found herself wondering. *What would it matter if it was someone else who filled the metallic soul-vehicle?*

With her programming in place she could have the android make any decision she wanted—such was the perk of making it from scratch. She didn't need it to have her mental capacities or memories, or her drives and motivations; she could make it do *anything*.

"Listen," Greg said gently, "I know you have the drive. I know you found my room. What you saw in there—"

"You mean all that stuff that could have helped me—and our people. Why have you lied to me this whole time? Did you want to see me fail?"

"That's not it at all," he said, aggrieved. "I just didn't want the same thing to happen to you that happened to our ancestors."

Cece stared, confused, waiting for the justification of his treacherous lies.

He took a deep shuddering breath, and it looked as though years of fatigue had caught up with him in that single instant. "Our people..."

Cece noticed his internal struggle and suddenly felt guilty for how she had treated him. All she wanted was to talk like they used to. "No secrets, Greg. Please. If you owe me anything, you owe me that."

"That's the problem. I was once like you, and then...and then I was promoted to Tech Officer by the person who had tutored me, much like I have done for you. He passed the role to me, much like I hoped to one day pass it onto you..."

Me...Tech Officer?

Of course. How could she have been so blind? How had she never realized how much hope Greg had placed in her? A fog of malcontent spread throughout her thoughts. What other blatant things had she overlooked while glued to her work? She had been working so hard she had forgotten to step back and reflect, forgotten to make sure her life was still flowing in the direction she wanted.

What would it be like to be one of the council members, to control the future of technology in the Sanctuary, to get permanent access to Greg's secret room, to have the freedom to go outside whenever she wanted?

Becoming Tech Officer would have been the best thing that could have happened to her, but was it still? Would she still want the position after all that had happened? Was it even an option anymore?

Greg broke the thoughtful silence. "When I found the room, I locked myself away from the world for days at a time, reading and studying every ounce of information we had. By the end of it, I knew why our people had died."

"The Virus..."

"The Virus was only the effect, but it wasn't the cause." Greg took a deep breath, shook his head wearily. "We died because we became too smart—too knowledgeable about the world. We had advanced to a level where godlike power existed in the hands of those who had no understanding of it—no appreciation for the gift they wielded. They manipulated the fundamentals of DNA and atoms and physics like they were toys—like they were simply building blocks that could be arranged casually just to see what might happen."

"But *I* know what I'm doing," Cece pleaded.

"Maybe you do now, but only within the limitations I've restricted you to. I've made sure you couldn't learn more. But I could have taught you things as a child that you wouldn't have understood the impact of, and with your intelligence and determination—and with that knowledge—you might have released a Virus that could have killed everyone in the Sanctuary."

"But you can't just keep people stupid. How can we make good decisions, make life better, if we don't know what our options are? If we're kept in the dark about the things that make us who we are..."

"Would you want a gun in your parents hands if they had no idea how to use it?" Greg asked. "Do you think that would be safe?"

"No. They're—" A wave of understanding crashed into Cece. She understood why Greg had betrayed her now—understood, but couldn't be sure she agreed. Sure, the Guardians tended to be lazy and lacked the drive to better themselves, but was that because they were born that way—or was it because they were kept that way? She understood Greg's desire to protect her and the other Guardians, but she wondered if his actions had only made things worse. Couldn't there be rules that limited external actions but not minds? Couldn't they educate their people in a way that empowered them without making them dangerous?

"You see it now, don't you?" Greg muttered. "The knowledge our people had gained put them in a world where there were haves and have-nots—where some people could afford to live in the luxuries of advanced technology while others died from the simple lack of clean water. But eventually, those at the bottom got their hands on the powerful—and very dangerous—technology, and they decided to use it to balance the scales. But they wiped out humanity instead. When they launched their viruses, they thought they'd only be taking out the people at the top. They thought they could guide the future of humanity by controlling the anti-virus. But they lost control, because they didn't understand what they had created."

"But don't you think, maybe—just maybe—we can eventually advance to a point where we can provide for everyone? Where we can make it so no one has to be hungry or thirsty or in danger...a point where there's enough memory for all the robots and enough food and water for the humans, and no one feels the need to steal or kill."

Greg gave a wary laugh. "No. I don't think it's possible—not with that kind of information on the loose. That's why I've kept the secrets, Cece. Because once our people realize how much power there is, someone is going to want to control it. Hell...if Kensington knew what I knew, knew what was in that room, he'd already have us filling shifts to power some new toy of his, just like he already has us doing so he can fulfill his food addiction. But there's always someone like that, someone who will always try to use others to make their own life better once they discover it's possible. Once people know there's more to life, they can't be content with what they already have..."

"Well, you'll understand if I have to prove you wrong."

"I hope you do, Cece. I really do. But I don't think humans have it in 'em."

"But maybe androids do. Maybe that's what we're supposed to be. Maybe our next step of evolution is to become machines and make ourselves incapable of such thoughts. A body free from suffering, free from the need to step on others to prevent the pain brought on by our own weaknesses. That's what I'm fighting for—to put our species back on the path of progress."

"But you can do that *without* risking your life. Any mind can be inside that body and still carry out your commands, can still bring you back what it finds." Greg let out a long, drawn-out sigh. "Just think about what you're risking, Cece. Ask yourself if your death is worth knowing some machine is wandering around that thinks like you. Ask yourself if it's worth the devastation you'd cause to the people who care about you...people like Curtis, your parents—and me"

"Greg, I—"

Greg raised his hand to silence her. "Just think about it." He turned and left without another word.

CHAPTER THIRTEEN

For the first time in as long as she could remember, Cece put aside all productive thought; instead, she lay in bed, losing herself in its comfort and in the reflective musings that filled her mind. She hated wasting time on thought that didn't have a tangible result—that didn't gain her some practical edge in life—but Greg's words had assaulted her confidence. And now she was racked with malcontent, her mind crippled with a paralyzing indecisiveness.

She was torn.

With Curtis at her side and the new drive to learn from, her life had never had more potential, had never been better. And yet, she was about to risk losing it all. For what? For the pride of having her consciousness in a machine? Was that what it was—pride?

Greg had made a good point: she personally gained nothing by giving the android her consciousness; it would carry out its commands regardless of the mind and memories that resided in it.

But the thought of her consciousness experiencing the beautiful gift of life on the surface filled her with a warmth she couldn't explain. And any source of bliss in the mundane life of the Sanctuary, even if it was something as intangible as an abstract thought, was worth cultivating.

That's all it takes, Cece realized. *Thought is all I need to be happy.*

It was the only thing that had brought her happiness since her sister's death. If not for the goal—the thought—of one day completing the android, she wouldn't have woken every day filled with passion and ambition. It was the thought that had added purpose to life. Why couldn't the thoughts of the android walking the surface do the same thing?

She imagined the android roaming across an alien world filled by machines and the crumbling remnants of humanity. A world full of lost treasures, rich with the history of her people—a history that represented a future. *How ironic*, she thought, *the ability to go into the past and find the future.* She had read about cities where buildings threatened the clouds with their needle-like spires, and whose shadows still held the vestige of the millions of people who once swarmed below on foot or on bikes, in cars or trains. And anything that hadn't already been looted by the androids was free for the taking.

What things could a human find that an android would overlook or not care for? What would it be like to have her reading perch thirty stories high instead three, to watch the sun rise, to live every day without fear of what might come at night and without the need to return to the dark and oppressive Sanctuary? It wasn't a sanctuary, Cece realized; it was a prison, for both body and mind. It was a too-small cage for a winged soul, barren soil where no life could grow.

It was no longer the android Cece imagined roaming the world; it was herself. She thought of the thrilling sensations of making her way across the landscape, walking through valleys steeped by colossal mountains that were thick with foliage, navigating across raging rivers where bears might be fishing, where hawks might fly overhead...

The thought filled her with a profound yearning. There were likely hundreds of animals that roamed the surface that she had never seen before, creatures her books didn't cover and that weren't mentioned in the sparse and incomplete computer records the Guardians had. What endless wonders her mind could take in with no limit on memory, with no faulty algorithms in her human mind to diminish the awe of discovery. No matter how accurately the android could record its journey, there were things like beauty and the feeling of the wind and the sun that couldn't be translated. She could read about the outside world all she wanted, look at as many pictures and videos as she could get her hands on, but knowing about it would never be as good as the real thing; knowledge could never replace experience.

She wanted that unpredictably, wanted to experience that beautiful orchestra of activity the outside world provided, each vibratory note of matter delivering ever-streaming sensations through her body. It was so vast, so incomprehensible in any given moment; the earth couldn't be broken into a simple analysis like her machines.

The thought made her uncomfortable, fearful of the loss of control it implied...but at the same time awoke within her a grand appreciation for the infinite growth the world could provide her. However, it worried her to know that any bit of food she might eat, any molecule of air she might inhale, could be laced with a bacteria or virus that could render her dead in mere moments.

That was why humanity needed to evolve, that was why she needed to ensure they became machines. The planet's natural intelligence had shown humankind their flaw, had left only a small band of them to better understand the message it was relaying. In Cece's mind, the message was simple: the human body is weak, but technology can fix the problems that evolution has taken too long to right.

A new notion spread roots in her mind. What had been a seed of fantasy was growing into a tangible possibility—a plan. Gone was the question of whether to upload her mind or not, and in its place was a new question: to stay at the Sanctuary, or to brave the surface and join the android on its quest? It was the unintended solution to Greg's problem; she didn't *need* to upload her mind when she had a perfectly good one that could experience first hand.

The door to her room swung open and pulled Cece from her reverie.

Curtis stepped inside. His brow narrowed at the sight of Cece alone on her bed, quiet, and with nothing occupying her hands. "Is everything okay?" he asked gently.

Cece smiled, nodding. "Yeah. Just thinking."

"That's what scares me." Curtis took a seat on the edge of the bed. "What happened?"

"Greg came by earlier."

Curtis' eyes widened in panic. "He knows?"

Cece nodded.

"And...? Did he take the drive? Did he tell Kensington and Lucia?"

"Nope," Cece said. "He just wanted to talk."

"About...?" Silence filled the moment. "Cece. What's going on? You're never this quiet. What did Greg say to you?"

"He just got me thinking." Cece met his gaze with thoughtful eyes. "Have you ever thought about leaving? The Sanctuary, the valley...all of it. Just heading off into the world."

Curtis stiffened, looked as though he had just been struck in the face by absurdity. "No. Never. Why would I?" His dark eyes pierced into Cece. "Don't you even think about it. Not after all this time. You can't go... you—you'll die out there."

"Come with me then," Cece pleaded, a glimmer of hope in her tone. She placed her hand upon his thigh. "We could keep each other safe. And the android could protect us, too. The three of us. Think of everything we could see and do. We'd be the first humans in decades to explore the surface."

"Because exploring the surface isn't a smart thing to do. It's not safe."

"It will never be safe," Cece said, the words escaping from her subconscious without thought, from some hidden part of her. She realized how true the statement was, realized she could no longer let the excuse of safety hold her back. "But that's what makes us different than everyone else here, right? We don't let fear keep us from doing the things we want. If we're ever going to move forward, someone has to take the risk eventually. Why can't it be us?"

Curtis rubbed at his eyes as his face contorted in struggled thought. He rose suddenly, pacing, thinking. He stopped and shook his head. "No...*No*...we can't. We're thinkers, Cece, not soldiers or explorers. We don't know anything about the outside world or how to survive it."

"Who does then...Lucia? Greg? They're never going anywhere. There's no one else to do it, Curtis. You and I are probably the most capable humans left on the planet, and we're smart enough to figure things out as we go along. This is it, Curtis. This is our chance to be the spark that restarts humanity. Just think of the impact we could have."

Cece's mind flooded with blissful thoughts of the dead cities of the world alive with activity once more. It was possible—the two of them could make it so. Her and Curtis could pick out their favorite structure and use it as a research lab, as a base from which they could reawaken the genius technology of their ancestors and deliver their creations to the masses. Androids would come and see what they were doing, and they could work together to rebuild a city bit by bit. And maybe there were other humans out there, somehow, who might learn of their new Mecca and come to join.

She and Curtis would be like the wizards in her stories, experimenting with modern magic and bettering the world with endless streams of breakthrough discoveries. And when they were old, they could just move their minds safely into machines and continue their work. They could expedite millennia of evolution from within their immortal bodies.

"We won't have any impact if we're dead," Curtis said sharply, shattering the beautiful image in Cece's mind.

She returned his stern glare. "And we won't have any impact if we just rot away here, either. We're squandering the gifts we've earned."

"That's easy for you to say—your work is nearly complete. But you want me to walk away from everything I've poured myself into when I'm making so much progress. My work has the power to change the world just as much as your precious drives of information."

"But how close are you, really?"

"Closer than you give me credit for. Sure, it could be years, but I can't just sacrifice my progress for a suicide mission because I'm bored of living in this dreadful place."

"We can come back to get your stuff, and by then you'll know even more. Those drives of information could be the entire reason you're able to finish your work." Cece rose to stand face to face with Curtis and took his hands in hers. "And we would be together, too, you and I, sharing an amazing journey of discovery."

"It's just not worth it, Cece. Send out your android with its directions and we can stay *here*... together, and safe. You have enough on that drive to keep you busy forever, so why do you need more? Why do you need an adventure?" He squeezed her hand. "And this...us...there's potential here—don't you think? Don't you want to explore *that*? And what about your family...don't you care about what it will do to them to lose you?"

"It's not like I'm betraying them; I'm just not letting them control my future because they birthed me. I'm not going to sacrifice my happiness just because my life doesn't fit their plans, just because I'm not being what they want. I have to be honest with my needs, not theirs, and what I need is somewhere I can grow, somewhere I don't feel guilty for thinking for myself. I want to learn and have new experiences, Curtis. That's how we evolve. That's how we survive."

"But you can learn and experience and still stay here, you just refuse to believe it. Running away from here won't make your life any better. You'll just find yourself lost and struggling to survive, and you'll be all alone with no one to help."

"No," she whispered, shaking her head, "I won't be alone."

CHAPTER FOURTEEN

Cece readied the Kernal for a mind upload with a practiced yet trembling hand. She was confident in her decision, but every anxious moment was a poison to her nerves that refused to subside. And Curtis' explosion from her room hours earlier had done little to calm her already hectic mind.

They had decided to talk it over the next day after they each had time to think, but Cece knew the conversation would never take place. She had already made her choice, and Curtis had made it clear he stood in opposition to it. He had taken Greg's side on things, had tried to convince her to stay in the Sanctuary, to use another mind besides her own in the android.

But it had to be her mind—her consciousness. It was best that whatever psyche filled the android understood the importance of the mission; there had to be a passion to complete it rather than just a forced instinct to fulfill a hard-coded directive. It wouldn't be worth the drama to convince Kensington to let her have access to a different mind from the database anyway. And with her consciousness inside the android it would almost be like having her sister back.

Everyone always said they were so alike anyway.

She gave a final examination of the machine. The uploader was on and armed, running steadily for nearly an hour now and only one command away from starting the scan. The dome in which she would place her head taunted her like some impatient abyss, and she found herself surprised by her own hesitance, by her own fear. She breathed deeply, glancing fearfully at the neural-cap and bottle of scanning nanobots for the dozenth time.

It had seemed like such an easy decision when she thought no one cared about her, when there had been nothing to lose and everything to gain. But her relationships with Curtis and Greg had only grown through the struggles and arguments. Everything bad that had happened suddenly seemed like a glue that bonded them all closer together. After seeing how heavily her decision weighed on them, she had gained an understanding that other people feared her death—even if she didn't; that her absence would bring pain to the only ones she cared about.

The precious hard drive only increased the stakes. Now her death could also mean the end of humanity's forward movement for decades to come—maybe even forever. The drive and all knowledge of it could be locked away, and generations of unquestioning Guardians would be none the wiser. Nineteen years she had unknowingly been within ten feet of a secret stockpile of goods that could have revolutionized her life, and to find it had required a once in a lifetime discovery and a GPS tracking device. Would future generations be so lucky?

But it had taken risks to make it this far, and if she was going to continue to help humankind restore its rightful place in the universe, well...then she had to take more.

It has to be my mind, she told herself. *It has to be.*

Cece yanked the bandana from her head, bringing strands of her coffee-colored hair over her eyes. She brushed them away and slipped the cap over her head. With a deep breath she grabbed the bottle of nanobots, stared at it as though it were a bottle of poison filled with tiny malevolent beings set on her destruction. As much as she had used her ancestor's technology in the past, she had never before ingested it, and putting possibly-deteriorated nanobots in her bloodstream sounded like a bad idea; but it was part of the process, and if she wanted to go through with it she had little choice.

She downed the viscous substance. Her face tightened into a sour cringe. She moved to the side of the gurney that the android rested upon, stared down at the mismatched scraps of shaped metal that a copy of her mind might soon live inside.

The moment had arrived.

She trembled as she settled into the uploader, as her head came to rest inside the magnetic dome that would interact with the cap on her head and the bots in her bloodstream.

She glanced at the android that lay next to her, saw the walnut of her eyes staring back at her in the metallic mirror. She turned away, looked down at her own hands. A sensation washed over her, as though she could feel every cell in her body awaken—from the smallest of atoms to the entirety of her flesh. Each breath sent ripples of warmth through her, and she couldn't be sure if it was a product of the nanobots or the acknowledgment of her own mortality.

Soon, there would be two of her in the world—or none.

Would the new her have that same voice inside her head? Would it worry like hers? Would it question itself the same way she did? Would it have the same yearnings that she had?

Why were all these questions coming to her now?

More and more questions gathered in line, waiting their turn to assault her confidence. But rather than give into her malcontent, she reached over and slammed the enter key.

A low hum.

It grew louder and louder, melodic and enthralling. The droning sound was hypnotic, adding weight to her fluttering eyelids. She steeled her mind, willing it be strong during the stressful activity. She dedicated herself fully to the empowerment of her consciousness; she didn't know how her present thoughts might transfer, but she wanted to believe she could will her strength into the machine.

A beep.

The monotone noise spoke of trouble. It wasn't a beep, she realized, it was an alarm. She wanted to get up and diagnose the problem, but she couldn't move. She was locked in until the scan finished. She had to stay still. Unable to shift her head in the slightest, she tried to glance at the monitor using only her eyes. The display confirmed her worst fears. The temperature gauge was climbing, flashing red with anger as it threatened its upper threshold.

Something's wrong.

Time slowed as her mind grasped the importance of the moment. This was the vital moment where she decided her future. She could abort, could cancel the scan and likely never be able to do it again; or, she could hold still and risk her life for a complete upload.

Panic gripped her.

Although one movement could remove the risk, could stop the scan and the overheating, no part of her acknowledged that as a viable option. It was strange—to see a way out but still feel like she had no choice. It was her worst fear, to lose her ability to choose; but this was bigger than her.

All she could do was watch—watch as the machine overloaded.

A spark.

She heard it, then saw it: one of the ancient cords that connected the scanner to the terminal was frying under the heat. She hadn't thought to check the internal integrity of the wires. The crackling electric grew louder, more irritated. The temperature gauge surpassed its ceiling. It was molten-red.

She closed her eyes, unable to stand the sight any

longer.

Would anyone continue her work if she died, or would humanity and its legacy be buried with the Guardians?

Her muscles tensed to hold on as the machine began to shake violently.

She should have been more open with Curtis, should have apologized to Greg.

Would they understand?

Would Allison be waiting for her...somewhere...

Was there somewhere else?

Was this the end?

Was—

An explosion.

Blackness.

CHAPTER FIFTEEN

"Cece," a voice called out, gentle and imploring.

The voice was familiar, but...different.

"You're going to be okay," the voice continued. "I've got you."

Cold, hard hands gripped her sides and yanked her forward. The movement made her dizzy. She fell slumped onto sharp, bony shoulders that dug into her stomach. She jostled around from her carrier's quick movements. Another sweeping movement and she was on her back, cold steel pressing against her back and sending a welcome cooling sensation throughout her body. A smile tugged at her lips.

"Can you hear me?"

It was a woman's voice, worried and afraid.

"Mom?" Cece asked, her eyes fluttering in an attempt to open them against the harsh light. "Am I... what happened?"

"The uploader overheated. The surge overwhelmed your neurons."

That voice, Cece thought. *Who—?*

Cece worked her eyes open, her gaze darting around frantically through the haze, fighting to understand. "Did—did it work?"

The android leaned over her, its smooth artificial features shifting into a smile. "It did," the android said, in a voice that sounded nearly identical to Cece's, only now it was tinted in electrical overtones. "We did it."

CHAPTER SIXTEEN

Cece fought to stabilize her body against the shaking as she sat on the edge of the gurney. Her brain was still firing signals randomly from the stresses it endured during the upload, and her eyes flickered as she struggled to cope with the dull sensations.

Her expression was blank as she stared at her creation, at the machine she had dedicated the past half-dozen years of her life to. She admitted to herself she had never actually been sure that she could do it—if it was even possible—and so she couldn't be sure if what she saw was real, or just some hopeful hallucination.

Or perhaps she had died, had gone to the heaven Kensington had so often preached about? But if she was dead...

No. She felt alive. And the android looked so real...

She studied it through the visual fatigue that racked her senses, tried to decide if the metallic humanoid was tangible or some twisting of reality that had resulted from damage to her brain.

It stood stoically, though its fingers strummed a melodic beat on the gurney while its body swayed ever so slightly, like a human who couldn't quite sit still—like Cece.

The once crude-looking body created by exposed pistons and circuitry now seemed somehow life-like, as though the addition of a consciousness had breathed the true essence of existence into the metal framework. And that face...the sleek, smooth humanoid face that Cece had taken directly from a scrapper the Guardians had found before she was even born, looked so authentically human. Although it was not a unique face, was in fact a default design used by all androids, Cece could still see a reflection of her own emotions in its features.

The thin nanofiber eyelids blinked suddenly as it peered closer. "Are you okay, Cece? Is there something I can get you?"

She reached out to touch it, her fingers clawing hesitantly through the air, getting ever closer as she gained the courage to test the validity of her perception.

Flesh fingers touched cold steel.

Heavy breaths came and went as a smile slowly formed on her face.

"You're... you're alive..."

"And you are, too."

And I am, too.

I'm alive...

It's alive!

Cece shut upright, stumbled momentarily from the dizziness of the rushed movement. She had to test it, to know once and for all it worked. "What—what's your name?"

"Cece"

"And your favorite color?"

"Blue—like the sky."

Cece's smile widened. "And...and where did I find the hard drive Greg took from me? From us?"

"In the well originally, but most recently in the secret room behind his closet."

Cece's smile beamed as she bounced in place from her excitement.

IT WORKED!

She threw her arms around the android, squeezed it tightly. "It worked! I can't believe it worked...you're— you're real! You're alive!" She pulled away, looked it up and down once more. "I can't believe it," she said, head shaking, tears filling her eyes. "I can't believe it worked."

"It worked, Cece. And we're both alive—luckily."

Cece took one look at the smoldering chair she had sat in only an hour before and her mood sobered immediately. The scene showcased a level of devastation she shouldn't have survived. As she looked over the wreckage she worried that her heart was as callous as Curtis had joked about, for it wasn't the near-death experience that racked her core with melancholy, but rather the loss of the uploader, of one of the world's most sophisticated and important pieces of technology.

Once Cece was finished mourning the loss of the uploader, and after confirming she was void of any major injuries, she turned her attention away from the burnt ruins and toward the android's well-being.

With the care of a physician, she plugged her metallic twin into the—thankfully undamaged—main terminal of the Kernal, then used the same analytics program she had used hundreds of times in the past to test the android's functionality.

The body hadn't been damaged in the slightest, and to her great surprise, neither had the mind. As far as Cece could tell, the transfer of her consciousness was a complete success. Even her own mind was beginning to feel back to normal by the time she finished the examination.

"I think we're fine," she told the android after the tests were complete.

"Should we go look for the hard drive now?" the android asked.

Cece unhooked the diagnostic cords from their various connections to the android's body. "Soon. Very soon," she replied. But there was one more thing she had to do before anything else. "Are you okay with me calling you Allison?"

"But I am not Allison. I am you. I am Cece."

"I know. But I think that could get confusing. And from this point forward, you can be anyone you want to be. I am simply the template, but you are your own person now."

The android smiled, metal shifting into the same sly grin Cece gave to others. She nodded. "I understand. I will be Allison, but only to honor my...*our* sister."

Our sister. The truth reverberated through Cece. She had two sisters now: one that was dead and one that was a machine. But they *were* her sisters, no matter what state their bodies might be in. "To honor our sister," Cece said, nodding her agreement.

Allison grabbed one of the two backpacks that rested near the gurney. Cece smiled proudly when she noticed Allison had grabbed the backpack that had been specifically packed for the strong back of the android. It was a simple thing, but it hinted that even Cece's most recent memories—that of packing the bags—had successfully transferred.

Allison swung on the pack, then turned anxiously to Cece. "Are we ready to go look for the hard drive now?"

Cece realized she may have set the hard drive directive to too high a priority, and that it would get annoying to have such a singularly-minded companion. "Do you mind if I change a few of your settings really quick? I wasn't sure you'd have my mind when I set them originally, so there are a few things I should probably change."

"My directive priority is too high, isn't it?"

Cece nodded her agreement with a smile, feeling proud that Allison's insights were so closely mirroring her own.

"Then, yes. Please adjust the settings."

Cece plugged Allison back into the Kernal, punched in a quick number change to lower the priority for the hard drive, and the problem was fixed.

Then Cece was struck by the awkward realization that there was nothing left to do, nothing holding her back from her plan. Everything had happened so fast...was she ready?

The bags were packed, their location was known, and she knew Curtis' choice. She had all the books and tools she needed for the road, a fair supply of food, and Allison's body had a fully-charged battery that would last indefinitely as long as her solar panels were exposed to enough sun.

Cece looked around the room, wondered if she had forgotten anything. She stood staring for several moments, trying to come to terms with the fact that there was no reason to linger any longer. "Okay." She sighed. "Let's do it."

Cece suddenly realized that the broader shoulders and rigid body of Allison would make getting through the tunnel near impossible. They were going to have to use the main entrance; she could only hope the hack she had put in place would get them through.

Cece gave a few short instructions to Allison to improve their stealth through the Sanctuary, all of which were met with Allison's continual stream of 'I know'. Cece struggled to comprehend that this machine knew everything she did up to an hour ago.

They set out towards the hatch, quietly making their way through the halls. To avoid waking anyone up, they decided to take the wing that passed by the lounge rather than go through the barracks.

But as they neared the entrance to the lounge, Cece heard voices coming from inside, though too quiet to decipher. She hugged the wall of the hallway, inched closer until she could poke her head around the corner.

Her parents sat halfway across the lounge. They talked in hushed conversation and their features were twisted by worry and stress—expressions which Cece felt her parents only wore when they meant to discipline her. The sight awoke a deep paranoia. *They're talking about me,* Cece thought. *They have to be.*

She edged closer, tried to make out their words, but

try as she might she couldn't untangle their mumbled tones. After several tense moments, Cece realized it was a futile attempt.

This is it, she thought. *I have to go now. Before they see me.*

But she struggled to push herself forward. Her nerves refused to calm, and her breaths came in short gasps while her stomach twisted into knots. Everything she had ever known was about to be gone from her life, and only the unfamiliar lay ahead. The decision had been so easy when there were obstacles that made it seem unachievable, but now there was nothing to stop her. The only thing that could get in her way now was herself.

Or so she thought.

But what had already been one of the hardest decisions of her life only worsened when Greg and Curtis, locked in conversation, entered into the hallway. Silence overtook them as they came to a sudden stop, eyes wide at the sight of Cece and the android that stood next to her.

CHAPTER SEVENTEEN

Greg took a timid step forward. "You—you did it." He came closer, studying the android from head to toe. "It's incredible. Were there any problems?" He turned to Allison. "Can you hear me?"

"Yes," Allison responded, "I can hear you."

"Astounding," Greg muttered, features shifting into a grin of awed wonderment.

Curtis shook his head in confusion. "Cece, I don't, I don't understand...where are you going? What are those bags for?"

Her parents emerged from the lounge then. Cece's mother started to speak, then saw the android. She yelped and jumped back in fear.

"Easy, Laura," Greg said. "It's Cece's. There's nothing to worry about."

"Well what is she doing with it?" She turned to Cece. "What are doing with it?"

"She was about to leave," Curtis said, his expression tender with sadness.

Greg noticed the bags, turned to Cece with pleading eyes. "Just to do some tests on the surface, right?"

"I don't think so," Curtis said, and the edge of hurt in his tone cut Cece to her core. "You were about to leave for good, weren't you?"

All of those gathered brought their stares to bear on Cece as they awaited her response.

A rush of fear shot through her. In an instant she

imagined what would happen. They would detain her, lock her inside the Sanctuary until she grew old and died an unnecessary death. They would dismantle her creation—dismantle the hope for their species. They would imprison her with their words, make the guilt so crushing that she would be forced to turn her back on her quest—on her chosen path in life. She attempted to rally her resolve, to prepare a guard against whatever they may bring against her.

But instead, she felt a constriction in her chest, a twist of fear and sadness. She felt too vulnerable to shut them out. They were her loved ones, closer to her than any others, yet they stood opposite her like an enemy force. These adversaries, however, wore no armor, only masks of despondency—of rejection.

"Cece." Her father spoke her name gently. "You wouldn't..."

"She would," her mother added. "You were just going to leave without saying goodbye, weren't you? Weren't you?" Her face strained in the effort to hold back the sadness.

"After all we've done for you," her father added. "After all we've lost. Do we not deserve better?"

"I never meant—" Cece choked on the words. What could she say? How could she make them understand she didn't want to hurt anyone, that she was only trying to do what she thought was right. "It seemed easier this way. I'm not good at these kinds of things. The thought of telling you... I knew how hard it would be to walk away from all of you, from all I've known. I just thought..." She couldn't find the words.

"Did you...did you think?" Greg asked, the hurt in his tone was sharp and profound, cutting deeper than her parents' words. "I have been there for you every time. I looked the other way for you so many times. I taught you, raised you as if you were my own. And I thought maybe I had finally gotten through to you. I thought you understood why we were trying so hard to keep you from hurting yourself..."

"I did understand," Cece pleaded. *I really did,* she thought, and she wished Greg could find the ability to do the same. "But—" Her next words surprised even her. "I'm scared, okay. I'm having just as hard of a time accepting this as all of you. I don't know what's going to happen. But I do know that this is what I want. I *know* this is where my happiness lies. And I just wanted to avoid giving you all a chance to sway me from that, from what I already know in my heart is the right decision."

"And what about our hearts?" Curtis demanded. "Everyone showed up here because I asked them to, so we could figure out how we could help you, how we could make you happy here." He came face to face with Cece. "You told me we would talk about it tomorrow. You lied to me, Cece. I've never been anything but honest with you—and you led me on this whole time, simply to leave me behind like some toy you tired of. Did you ever care, or were you just using me?"

"Curtis..." Cece laid a hand upon his arms. "I never lied to you. Everything we've talked about was from my heart. And how can you think I led you on? We had only just started—"

Curtis pulled away, shaking his head in disbelief.

Cece felt stranded. "I asked you to come with me!" she blurted, the pain of abandonment adding an edge to her words. "I asked all of you to support me in my decision."

"But your decision is too damn dangerous," Greg cut in. "We're trying to keep you safe."

"No!" Frustration raked her senses. "No. No, you're all trying to make me into what you want. You're all laying your fears on my shoulders. I'm not like you. I'm not scared to question our existence. I'm not afraid to move forward. Don't punish me because I have the courage to want more out of my life. Any of you can come with me."

She gestured to Allison. "With us. You don't have to stay confined to this prison either. We can all explore together. As friends, as family—" She turned to Curtis. "As lovers..."

Profound sadness weighed on Curtis' features, and his body sagged in desperation. "This is our home, Cece. *All* of ours—you included. Why can't we stay here?" He gestured toward Allison. "Let your machine do the dangerous stuff; and we can stay here, happy and safe."

Tears rimmed Cece's eyes, but her head seemed unable to resist shaking its defiance. Several long and tender moments passed, then finally she found the words that could deliver her entire defense: "But I'm not happy here," she said with sad finality. She turned to the machine at her side, the only friend she had left. Her sister. "Come on, Allison. I think it's time we go."

"Allison?" her mother blurted, face contorting with red hot anger. "How dare—"

"Enough!" Cece's dad exploded. "She's made her decision. This is her life. We have to let her go."

Cece stiffened at her father's words, stared at him with a shocked appreciation. She never loved her father as much as she did in that moment, which only made her next decision harder. "Thank you," she whispered to him. "If any of you want to join me, you're welcome. But I've got to go now. I can't... I can't stay."

She looked into each of their eyes, into the infinite unspoken words reflected there. None of them had words for that moment. She contemplated staying, of looking for a new solution, but she knew it would be choosing a lie. *I will not lie to myself,* she thought. And with a final smile that said 'thank you' to each of them, she pressed through their ranks and continued on.

"Are you ever coming back?" Curtis asked. "Or do you plan to leave us behind forever?"

Cece stopped, turned to face him. "I don't know. But I hope we'll see each other again."

They stared at each other for several long moments, both unwilling to compromise, both wanting nothing more than to compromise.

"Goodbye," Cece finally muttered, then turned and rounded the corner, making her way to the locked door.

Although she would have thought it was impossible, she became even more terrified as she realized she still had one more obstacle left. And if her untested passcode failed, she would have to face the heartbreaking task of looking into Greg's sad eyes and asking for his help one last time.

She went to the keypad and punched in the code with trembling fingers: 0 0 0 0 0 1 0.

Nothing.

She waited, head shaking angrily at the lock, her face tightening to hold back the pressure of tears that wanted to flow freely, her checks hurting from the effort.

Come on, Come on, Come on, she pleaded with her thoughts.

The keypad flashed suddenly, lost all power momentarily, then lit up with power once more. The mechanical locked clicked and the door released a whisper of wind as it unsealed. She felt too numb to celebrate.

Cece solemnly made her way through and grabbed onto the ladder that would lead her out through the hatch and onto the surface above—to her future.

As she climbed, each rung of the ladder seemed farther out of reach than the one before it. She fought against the guilt that pulled her downward, battled its ferocity with the lightness of love—love for life and love for truth. She had to be true to herself.

And if those below loved her like she loved them, they would understand. They would understand that sometimes following your heart may appear selfish, but that in the end it's better for everyone.

Dawn was breaking as she climbed from the hatch, arriving in the shadow of the water tower overhead.

Allison emerged at her side, and after a long moment of hesitation they moved off toward the twilight of the horizon.

"We're doing the right thing," Allison told her. "Your memories and my calculations have shown me as much."

"I hope you're right," Cece said. But as she thought of those people she was leaving behind, she wondered if the most logical choice was always the right one.

ABOUT THE AUTHOR

Steven Parton was born and raised in a small town in rural Ohio. With little variation in the stories told by the vast cornfields that surrounded him, he used the stories held within literature, film, and video games to fuel his imagination instead.

His fascination with the human condition and technology eventually led him to study Computer Science at University, where he simultaneously cultivated a healthy obsession with psychology and eastern philosophy.

After graduating, he spent two years traveling before deciding to settle in Portland, OR. When not writing, he enjoys biking, traveling, philosophizing, and partaking in food and cheer and all things geeky.

He likes to write stories that challenge the reader to examine social and philosophical issues, while also providing an immersive and exciting world to explore. He believes there is nothing more important than cultivating self while loving all that life brings your way, but that one should never forget to laugh either.

Also available from

Curious Apes Publishing:

The Evolution of Strangers

By Jonathon S. Kendall

Saudade

By Donovan James